LORD OF THE TREES

PHILIP JOSÉ FARMER

LORD OF THE TREES

VOLUME X OF
THE MEMOIRS OF LORD GRANDRITH
EDITED BY PHILIP JOSÉ FARMER

TITAN BOOKS

LORD OF THE TREES
Print edition ISBN: 9781781162934
E-book edition ISBN: 9781781162941

Published by Titan Books
A division of Titan Publishing Group Ltd
144 Southwark St, London SE1 0UP

First edition: November 2012
1 3 5 7 9 10 8 6 4 2

LORD OF THE TREES

A TALE OF TWO UNIVERSES

INTRODUCTION BY WIN SCOTT ECKERT

Philip José Farmer's novels of the Nine, *A Feast Unknown* (1969), *Lord of the Trees* (1970), and *The Mad Goblin* (1970) (all part of Titan Books' Wold Newton series under the subheading "Secrets of the Nine—Parallel Universe"), recount the ongoing battle of the ape-man Lord Grandrith and the man of bronze Doc Caliban against the Nine, a secret cabal of immortals bent on amassing power and manipulating the course of world events. These novels present an interesting conundrum for followers of Farmer's Wold Newton mythos.

Farmer wrote two biographies which kicked off the Wold Newton Family in earnest after he wrote the Nine novels: *Tarzan Alive: A Definitive Biography of Lord Greystoke* (1972) and *Doc Savage: His Apocalyptic Life* (1973; revised 1975). In these biographies, he uncovered the true identities of the men whose adventures had been presented to the world in the guise of popular fiction under the fabricated names "Lord Greystoke" and "Doc Savage."

And the true identities Farmer revealed were *not* John Cloamby, Lord Grandrith, and Doctor James Caliban, despite having written the Nine novels just a few years earlier, sourced directly from Grandrith's and Caliban's memoirs.

Instead, "Lord Greystoke's" real name remains undisclosed (although there are many hints in the strands and threads presented in *Tarzan Alive*), while "Doc Savage's" real name is Doctor James Clarke Wildman, Jr.

Furthermore, the backgrounds of Greystoke and Grandrith, and of Wildman and Caliban, are bursting with significant similarities and noteworthy differences.

Greystoke and Grandrith are both feral men. Both were born after their parents were shipwrecked off the coast of Gabon, were raised by sub-humans or "great apes," and went on to become "Wild Men of the Jungle," discover secret sources of gold, and have many wondrous adventures. Both men have similar Apollo-like physiques, are about six-foot-two-inches tall, and have coal-black hair and gray eyes.

Both jungle lords have "biographers," the term Grandrith uses when referring to the man who wrote a series of highly fictionalized novels and stories about him for popular consumption. Grandrith then goes one better than his biographer, writing his own autobiographical memoirs, of which *A Feast Unknown* is Volume IX and *Lord of the Trees* is Volume X.

As for Greystoke, Philip José Farmer followed in the footsteps of the jungle lord's original biographer with a more realistic account of his adventures, *Tarzan Alive*, as well as two novels presented as fiction, *The Peerless Peer* and *The Dark Heart of Time: A Tarzan Novel.*

Greystoke was born on November 22, 1888, a few minutes after midnight. Grandrith was born on November 21, 1888, at 11:45 p.m.

Both are immortal.

Greystoke's immortality was conferred by a grateful witch doctor. The month-long process involved a vile brew of herbs and a blood transfusion. The one-time procedure resulted in eternal youth.

Grandrith's immortality came from annual visits to the secret caverns of the Nine, somewhere in Africa, where "candidates" participated in a ceremony requiring the painful removal and consumption of certain parts of flesh. The Nine's elixir caused the regrowth of any lost organs and tissue. The immortality elixir could extend life to as much as 30,000 years before death due to old age.

Unlike the two jungle lords, Wildman and Caliban are "Men of the Metropolis," of science and technology. They are champions of justice. Both have bronzed skin and hair, and are about six-foot-eight-inches tall. They were each raised by their fathers, in a bizarre training program, to the height of physical and mental perfection, with the goal of fighting evildoers all over the world. Both men are geniuses, surgeons at the top of their field, and world-class experts in a variety of disciplines and sciences, including biology, engineering, physics, archeology, chemistry, law, and more. Both are responsible for inventions and scientific breakthroughs far beyond their time.

Wildman and Caliban each battled criminals with the aid of a band of five adventurers, beginning in the 1930s. Both men had cousins named Patricia. James Wildman's cousin was Pat

"Savage" (or really, "Wildman," as Farmer discovered), while James Caliban's cousin was Trish Wilde.

Both men, of course, are nicknamed "Doc."

As with Greystoke and Grandrith, Wildman's and Caliban's adventures were fictionalized in pulp magazine stories. There was no mention of sex in these, but *A Feast Unknown* reveals that Doc Caliban had an ongoing (if repressed) sexual relationship with his cousin Trish Wilde. Farmer speculates on Doc Wildman's sexuality in *Doc Savage: His Apocalyptic Life*, but firm information comes from his novel *The Evil in Pemberley House* (coauthored with Win Scott Eckert) wherein we discover that he has a daughter, Patricia Wildman, born in 1950, who takes after her father in many respects.

James Clarke Wildman, Jr., was born on November 12, 1901. James Caliban was born in 1903 (*A Feast Unknown*) or 1901 (*The Mad Goblin*). The 1901 date makes more sense, as Grandrith mentions in *Lord of the Trees* that Caliban fought in the Great War: "...he served with distinction as a commissioned officer in the U.S. Army in 1918." And in *The Mad Goblin*, it's noted that, "When Doc was only seventeen and a lieutenant in World War I, he had captured two German soldiers at the same time that he had been cut off by the advance of the enemy."

In *A Feast Unknown*, Grandrith spied upon Caliban's elderly aides, the dapper Mr. Rivers and the apish Mr. Simmons, and learned from them the 1903 date. We can assume they misspoke, or he misheard them.

Of course, seventeen is underage, but many who fought had enlisted before the age of eighteen. Doc Wildman certainly did, entering the Great War as a combat pilot at the age of sixteen, as outlined in Farmer's *Escape from Loki: Doc Savage's First Adventure.*

Farmer speculated that Doc Wildman had access to an immortality elixir in the form of *Kavuru* pills discovered by his relative, Greystoke. Doc Caliban was also a candidate of the Nine and beholden to that secret organization in exchange for the same immortality elixir as Grandrith used.

The source of Grandrith's and Caliban's strength, intelligence, physical perfection, and extraordinary abilities differs from that of Greystoke and Wildman. The latter two are inheritors of the Wold Newton gene, reinforced in them by generations of intermarriage.

As for half-brothers Lord Grandrith and Doc Caliban, their amazing capabilities and talents derive from their grandfather, the immortal member of the Nine called XauXaz, inserting himself into the family line many times over. Since Grandrith and Caliban are the grandsons of a Cro-Magnon man, their bones are much larger and have a much greater surface area for muscle attachment.

Grandrith also believes that XauXaz's brothers, Ebn XauXaz and Thrithjaz, contributed to the Grandrith family line in a similar fashion, and that Castle Grandrith may have been used by the Nine, or some members of the Nine, as a breeding farm. It is strongly implied that the Grandrith lineage is the result of an elaborate eugenics program, carried out by the Nine over the millennia.

Grandrith's and Caliban's genealogies also differ from those of Greystoke and Wildman.

Lord Grandrith's father is actually the man known to

the world as his uncle: John Cloamby. His legal father, James Cloamby, Viscount Grandrith, is actually his uncle, although the Viscount was married to Grandrith's mother, Alexandra Applethwaite. John Cloamby, in the madness brought on by the Nine's elixir, raped his sister-in-law Alexandra, resulting in pregnancy and the birth of Lord Grandrith, the jungle lord. The mad John Cloamby also became the serial killer known as Jack the Ripper.

Later, the madness subsided and John Cloamby escaped to America, changed his surname to Caliban, became a doctor, and fathered James Caliban.

The real father of John and James Cloamby, and their brother Patrick Cloamby, was XauXaz of the Nine. Patrick Cloamby was the father of Trish Wilde; he preceded his brother John to America after assaulting and almost killing a teacher (presumably under the influence of the elixir), also became a doctor, and changed his surname to Wilde in order to escape his past. Trish Wilde was born in 1911.

We know much more about Greystoke's and Wildman's genealogies, which have been extensively traced by Philip José Farmer and documented as the Wold Newton Family in two essays: "A Case of a Case of Identity Recased, or, *The Grey Eyes Have It*" (published as an addendum to *Tarzan Alive*) and "The Fabulous Family Tree of Doc Savage (Another Excursion into Creative Mythography)" (published as an addendum to the biography *Doc Savage: His Apocalyptic Life*).

The Wold Newton Family genealogy is far too extensive and tangled to cover in depth here, but from these tracts we know that Greystoke and Wildman are kin (they are cousins, sharing the same great-grandfather, among other relations), and are also closely related to many other crimefighters, adventurers, geniuses, and criminal masterminds. These extraordinary people all share the Wold Newton gene, which is reinforced to different degrees based on the amount of intermarriage in their backgrounds.

The Wold Newton mutation occurred when the Wold Cottage meteor struck on December 13, 1795, exposing seven couples and their coachmen to the ionized radiation of the meteor. They "were riding in two coaches past Wold Newton, Yorkshire... A meteorite struck only twenty yards from the two coaches... The bright light and heat and thunderous roar of the meteorite blinded and terrorized the passengers, coachmen, and horses... They never guessed, being ignorant of ionization, that the fallen star had affected them and their unborn." (*Tarzan Alive*, Addendum 2, pp. 247–248.) This was "the single cause of this nova of genetic splendor, this outburst of great detectives, scientists, and explorers of exotic worlds, this last efflorescence of true heroes in an otherwise degenerate age." (*Tarzan Alive*, Addendum 2, pp. 230–231.)

Farmer discovered that many other well-known people are part of the Wold Newton Family. A short list includes: Solomon Kane (a pre-meteor strike ancestor); The Scarlet Pimpernel (present at the meteor strike); Fitzwilliam Darcy and his wife, Elizabeth Bennet (present at the meteor strike); Sherlock Holmes and his foe Professor Moriarty (aka Captain Nemo); Phileas Fogg; A.J. Raffles; the evil Fu Manchu and his archrival, Sir Denis Nayland Smith; Sir Richard Hannay; Lord Peter Wimsey; The Shadow; Sam Spade; Doc Savage's friend and associate Monk Mayfair, his cousin Pat Savage, and his daughter Patricia Wildman; The Spider; Nero Wolfe (the son of Sherlock Holmes); The Avenger; Philip Marlowe; James Bond; Travis McGee; and many others.

As I noted in the afterword to Farmer's *The Other Log of Phileas Fogg* (Titan Books, 2012), his researches are extremely well-sourced, including a personal interview with the jungle lord and countless hours spent poring over *Burke's Peerage*. Following the Greystoke and Wildman biographies, Farmer related adventures of the Wold Newton Family in the guise of fiction, similarly sourced from newly discovered, or unpublished, manuscripts and diaries.

Which brings us to the conundrum I noted at the beginning of this introduction.

The prior publication of the Nine novels *A Feast Unknown*, *Lord of the Trees*, and *The Mad Goblin* have created the idea in some readers that the Wold Newton biographies, novels, and stories are all works of fiction. After all, the first two novels are also sourced from the memoirs of Lord Grandrith, and edited for publication by Farmer. *The Mad Goblin* was written by Doc Caliban in the third person singular, though again it is autobiographical and Farmer edited it for publication.

Farmer claims, in essence, that both the Wold Newton stories and the Nine novels are true. They are all—or almost all—based on the accounts of the men and women who experienced the adventures and survived to tell the tales. Or they are sourced from manuscripts, memoirs, and diaries left behind by those who lived through amazing exploits.

However, some readers have concluded that it all must

be fiction—make-believe, the result of Farmer's overactive imagination—because the Wold Newton tales and the Nine novels appear to be mutually exclusive, based on the differing accounts and histories as outlined above.

There are several potential explanations for the apparent discrepancies. Perhaps the Nine novels are highly fictionalized adventures of the real Greystoke and Savage. Farmer published the books before discovering and revealing the true backgrounds of these men in *Tarzan Alive* and *Doc Savage: His Apocalyptic Life*. In this scenario, Wold Newton novels such as *The Other Log of Phileas Fogg*, *Time's Last Gift*, *The Peerless Peer*, the Khokarsa series (*Hadon of Ancient Opar*, *Flight to Opar*, and *The Song of Kwasin*), *Ironcastle*, *Escape from Loki*, *The Dark Heart of Time*, and *The Evil in Pemberley House* are truer reflections of the lives of these heroes.

In this set-up, Farmer's initial meeting with "James Claymore" (the putative John Cloamby) at the home of a mutual friend in Kansas City, Missouri, as recounted by Farmer in his "Editor's Note" to *A Feast Unknown*, is a falsehood created by Farmer to lend legitimacy to his manuscript. Perhaps Farmer had stumbled upon rumors and half-truths regarding the events of *A Feast Unknown*, *Lord of the Trees*, and *The Mad Goblin*, and had crafted these into a rousing adventure trilogy. If so, Farmer may have been embarrassed when he actually met the real Greystoke a few years later, although it's not clear from their interview that the two men discussed the incident.[1]

---

[1] "An Exclusive Interview with Lord Greystoke." (Originally published as "Tarzan Lives" in *Esquire*, April 1972; reprinted in Farmer's *Tarzan Alive: A Definitive Biography of Lord Greystoke*, University of Nebraska Press Bison Books, 2006.)

Alternatively, Lord Grandrith's and Doc Caliban's escapades could have occurred much as Farmer documented them, based on these supermen's memoirs. In this scenario, the two heroes coexist alongside their more famous analogues in the Wold Newton Universe. Farmer scholar Dennis E. Power is a proponent of this theory, and has outlined his thoughts in an intricate series of interconnected articles on his website, *The Wold Newton Universe: A Secret History* (pjfarmer.com/secret/index.htm). Briefly, Power suggests that Grandrith and Caliban are the result of an elaborate plan by the Nine to create doppelgängers of Greystoke and Wildman.

Power, discussing Grandrith and Caliban vis-à-vis the Wold Newton Family, suggests that, "Although the characters of Doc Caliban and Lord Grandrith can be placed in the Wold Newton Universe, we must ask if they were members of the Wold Newton Family. I would doubt that they were immediately related to the Wold Newton line, but a relationship possibly exists. Farmer claimed that [Greystoke] was descended from Odin. In all three of the Doc Caliban/Lord Grandrith novels, the claim is made that XauXaz was Odin. If not all of XauXaz's families and progeny were designated for the Nine's breeding programs, then it is a possibility that he was a distant ancestor to Greystoke and [Doc Wildman]."

Under this scenario, Farmer met Cloamby (as "James Claymore") much as described in *A Feast Unknown*, and was later put in touch with Caliban, serving as the editor of their manuscripts. A few years later he met and interviewed Greystoke.

A third explanation is that Lord Grandrith and Doc Caliban exist in a universe which is parallel, but very similar, to the Wold

Newton Universe. This alternate universe may share a common past with the Wold Newton Universe, but perhaps diverged from it at some point in the distant millennia. Or perhaps the two universes have always been parallel and coexistent.

The parallel universe theory is supported by Farmer's fragment of a fourth Nine novel, *The Monster on Hold*. The fragment was introduced by Farmer at the 1983 World Fantasy Convention, and was published in the convention program.[2] During a series of adventures in which Doc Caliban continues to battle the forces of the Nine, he "begins to suffer from a recurring nightmare and has dreams alternating with these in which he sees himself or somebody like himself. However, this man, whom he calls The Other, also at times in Caliban's dreams seems to be dreaming of Caliban."

Later, when Caliban has descended below the surface into a labyrinthine series of miles-deep caverns, in search of the extra-dimensional entity known as Shrassk, a being which had been invoked and then imprisoned by the Nine in the eighteenth century, Caliban has another vision of The Other: "The Other was standing at the entrance to a cave. He was smiling and holding up one huge bronze-skinned hand, two fingers forming a V."

"One huge bronze-skinned hand."

The Other is Doc Wildman, communicating to Caliban across the dimensional void.

---

[2] Reprinted in *Myths for the Modern Age: Philip José Farmer's Wold Newton Universe*, Win Scott Eckert, ed., MonkeyBrain Books, 2005; and in *Pearls from Peoria*, Paul Spiteri, ed., Subterranean Press, 2006. An additional fragment of the novel, entitled "Down to Earth's Centre," has since been located in Mr. Farmer's "Magic Filing Cabinet," and was published in *Farmerphile: The Magazine of Philip José Farmer* no. 12, Paul Spiteri and Win Scott Eckert, eds., April 2008.

Dennis Power takes a different view: "In this fragment, Farmer seemed to indicate that Doc Caliban and the Nine lived in an alternate universe from [Doc Wildman]. While Shrassk, the… monster, was most likely extra-dimensional, Doc Caliban of course was not, although he may have become trapped in other-dimensional space by the machinations of the Nine. I think that Farmer may have made the assertion that Doc Caliban, Grandrith, etc., resided in a different universe for a few reasons. First of all was the safety of his family. Having learned that the Nine were not entirely wiped out, he wanted to demonstrate that he was not a threat to them. By placing them in another universe, it is as if he was saying that not only were they fictional, but also that no true life counterparts ever existed in the real world. Also, he may have been trying to forever end the controversial theory that Grandrith and Caliban were [Greystoke] and [Doc Wildman]. This theory still raises the hackles today among casual readers of Farmer's works who have only read *A Feast Unknown*, *Lord of the Trees*, or *The Mad Goblin*, and not his biographies or authorized novels about the real [Greystoke] and Doc."

Nonetheless, if one disagrees with Power, the parallel universe explanation begs the question how Farmer came into possession of Grandrith's memoirs.

Could Farmer have received Grandrith's and Caliban's manuscripts from an alternate universe? Assuming that Farmer's recounting of meeting Grandrith in Kansas City is accurate—at least from Farmer's perspective—how might this have occurred? And how did Grandrith subsequently deliver Volume X of his memoirs (which became *Lord of the Trees*) to Farmer? How did Farmer receive Doc Caliban's manuscript for *The Mad Goblin*?

Perhaps Grandrith learned how to cross the dimensional gate and delivered his manuscripts and that of Caliban to a noted writer of science-fiction in an alternate universe who would understand it? Probably not, as Doc Caliban does not seem to have any knowledge of the parallel universe in 1977 and 1984 (the dates of the two known fragments of Caliban's further adventures, "Down to Earth's Centre" and *The Monster on Hold*); presumably, if Grandrith had learned to traverse the dimensions in the late 1960s, he would have informed his half-brother Caliban.

Could someone else have passed through the dimensional gate and given the manuscript to Farmer? It would not have been hard to pose as Lord Grandrith (or rather, "James Claymore") during their one meeting, since Farmer had never met him, and indeed had never heard of him. But Farmer, with his fascination with Edgar Rice Burroughs' tales of a jungle lord raised by "apes," would have been instantly hooked by the story of a real-life feral man brought up under such unusual circumstances, and it would not have been hard to convince him that Grandrith was the real-life inspiration for Burroughs' tales—which, in fact, was largely true; they just happened to be Burroughs' tales in an alternate universe.

Much later, when Doc Caliban conveyed to Farmer the events of *The Monster on Hold*—presumably Caliban later learned how to travel across the dimensional nexus held open by Shrassk—Farmer realized he had been duped back in the late 1960s. Or at least partially duped. For the man who had delivered the manuscripts to him had not been Lord Grandrith, but someone who had had other reasons for making the manuscripts public in Farmer's universe.

The presence of Doc Wildman in the caverns deep beneath New England, at the gate held open by the Shrassk entity, as observed by Doc Caliban across the dimensional nexus, strongly indicates that there also exists a secret organization of the Nine in Farmer's universe (i.e., Wildman and Greystoke's dimension, known as the Wold Newton Universe). Depending on whether the two universes diverged at some common point in the distant past, or whether they have always been coexistent, the Nine in each universe might conceivably have some members in common, members who were alive when the universes divided.

Or, the makeup of the Nine could be completely different in each universe.

Either way, if one of the Nine learned how to cross the dimensions, he may have posed as Lord Grandrith and delivered the manuscript for *A Feast Unknown* to Farmer with the intent of causing much disruption and consternation among the members of the Nine in the Wold Newton Universe. These members of the Nine, upon reading *A Feast Unknown* (for surely the book would be quickly brought to their attention and they would intently analyze it) would recognize much of themselves, and would also see a great many differences, but the overriding questions posed among them would be *how?* and *why?*

It would take someone of a Trickster's mentality to conceive of such a stunt. Someone with a long reputation for causing chaos, someone who is capricious and cunning, someone who changes his shape—or changes identities—as easily as others change their clothing.

As Christopher Paul Carey pointed out, when discussing *Escape from Loki: Doc Savage's First Adventure* in his "The Green

Eyes Have It—Or Are They Blue? Or, Another Case of Identity Recased,"[3] "One thing is for certain, and that is that [Baron] von Hessel presented himself to Doc in the role of the Norse All-father god Odin to Doc's Siegfried. Odin is the cynical god who gave up his left eye for a look at the future."

One member of the immortal Nine fits this description,' and in fact is understood to be the person who was the historical basis for Odin: XauXaz.

Of course, as the 1968 events of *A Feast Unknown* unfold, XauXaz is recently deceased.

Deceased in the Nine's Universe, at any rate.[4]

Win Scott Eckert

Denver, Colorado

July 2012

Win Scott Eckert is the coauthor with Philip José Farmer of the Wold Newton novel The Evil in Pemberley House, *about Patricia Wildman, the daughter of a certain bronze-skinned pulp hero (Subterranean Press, 2009). In 1997, he launched the first Wold Newton website,* The Wold Newton Universe *(www.pjfarmer. com/woldnewton/Pulp.htm). He is the editor of and contributor to* Myths for the Modern Age: Philip José Farmer's Wold Newton Universe *(MonkeyBrain Books), a 2007 Locus Awards finalist. He*

---

[3] *Myths for the Modern Age: Philip José Farmer's Wold Newton Universe*, Win Scott Eckert, ed., MonkeyBrain Books, 2005.

[4] For more on this, see the Wold Newton Origins tale "The Wild Huntsman" by Win Scott Eckert in *The Worlds of Philip José Farmer 3: Portraits of a Trickster*, Michael Croteau, ed., Meteor House, 2012.

has also coedited three *Green Hornet* anthologies for Moonstone Books, and his short fiction about adventurous characters such as Zorro, *The Green Hornet, The Avenger, The Phantom, The Scarlet Pimpernel, Hareton Ironcastle, The Green Ghost, Honey West, T.H.E. Cat, Captain Midnight, Doc Ardan,* and Sherlock Holmes, can be found in the pages of various anthologies from Moonstone Books and Black Coat Press. His critically acclaimed, encyclopedic Crossovers: A Secret Chronology of the World 1 & 2 . .; recently released by Black Coat Press. His latest project is the Wold Newton Origins series of interconnected short stories found in several volumes of Meteor House's annual anthology The Worlds of Philip José Farmer. *Win holds a B.A. in Anthropology, a Juris Doctorate, and lives with his wife Lisa and a menagerie of three cats and two dogs near Denver, Colorado. Find him on the web at www.winscotteckert.com.*

EDITOR'S NOTE
BY PHILIP JOSÉ FARMER

Although the editors of this book insist upon publishing this work as a novel under my by-line, it is actually Volume X of the Memoirs of Lord Grandrith, as edited by me for publication. The British spellings and the anglicisms of Lord Grandrith have been changed by me for an easier understanding by American readers.

The location of the caves of the Nine and several other places have purposely been made inexact. This is for the benefit of any reader who might try to find these places.

The Nine must have marked me off as dead beyond doubt.

I don't know whether or not the pilot of the fighter jet saw me fall into the ocean. If he did, he probably did not fly down for a closer look. He would have assumed that, if the explosion of my amphibian did not kill me, the fall surely would. After hurtling twelve hundred feet, I should have been smashed flat against the surface of the Atlantic off the coast of the West African nation of Gabon. The waters would be as hard as Sheffield steel when my body struck.

If the pilot had known that men had survived falls from airplanes at even greater heights, he might have swooped low over the surface just to make certain that I was not alive. In 1942, a Russian fell twenty-two thousand feet without a parachute into a snow-covered ravine and lived. And other men have fallen two thousand feet or higher into water or snow and lived. These were freak occurrences, of course.

The pilot would have reported that the twin-engine

propellered amphibian I was flying to the *Parc National du Petit Loango* had gone up in a ball of flame at the first pass. The .50 caliber machine guns or rockets or whatever he had used had hit the fuel tanks and burning bits of wreckage had scattered everywhere. Among the bits was my body.

I recovered consciousness a few seconds later. Blue was screaming around me. My half-naked body was as cold as if the wind were ripping through my intestines. The explosion had ripped off most of my clothing or else they had been torn off when I went through the nose of the craft. I was falling toward the bright sea, though, at first I sometimes thought I was falling toward the sky. I whirled over and over, seeing the rapidly dwindling silvery jet speeding inland and the widely dispersed and flaming pieces describing smoky arcs.

I also saw the white rim of surf and flashing white beaches and, beyond, the green of the bush jungle.

There was no time or desire to think ironic thoughts then, of course. But if there had been, I would have thought how ironic it was that I was going to die only a few miles from my birthplace. If I had thought I was going to die, that is. I was still living, and until the final moment itself that is what I will always tell myself. *I live.*

I must have fallen about two hundred feet when I succeeded in spreading out my legs and arms. I have done much sky diving for fun and for survival value. It was this that enabled me to flatten out and gain a stable attitude. I was slowing down my rate of descent somewhat by presenting as wide an area as possible to the air, acting as my own parachute. And then I slipped into the vertical position during the last fifty feet, and I entered the water like a knife with my hands forming the knife's tip.

I struck exactly right. Even so, the impact knocked me out. I awoke coughing saltwater out of my nose and mouth. But I was on the surface, and if I had any broken bones or torn muscles, I did not feel them.

There was no sign of the killer plane or of my craft. The sky had swallowed one and the sea the other.

The shore was about a mile away. Between it and me were the fins of at least two sharks.

There wasn't much use trying to swim around the sharks. They would hear and smell me even if I made a wide detour. So I swam toward them, though not before I had assured myself that I had a knife. Most of my clothing had been ripped off, but my belt with its sheathed knife was still attached to me. This was an American knife with a five-inch blade, excellent for throwing. I left it in the sheath until I saw one of the fins swerve and drive toward me. Then I drew it out and placed it between my teeth.

The other fin continued to move southward.

The shark may have just happened to turn toward me in the beginning, but an increase of speed showed that it had detected me. The fin stayed on the surface, however, and turned to my right to circle me. I swam on, casting glances behind me. It was a great white shark, a species noted for attacking men. This one was wary; it circled me three times before deciding to rush me. I turned when it was about twenty feet from me. The surface water just ahead of it boiled, and it turned on its side just before trying to seize my leg. Or perhaps it only intended to make a dry run to get a closer look at what might be a dangerous prey.

I pulled my legs up and stabbed at it with both hands

holding the hilt of the knife. The skin of the shark is as tough as cured hippo hide and covered with little jags—placoid scales—that can tear the skin off a man if he so much as rubs lightly against it. My only experience in fighting sharks was during World War II when my boat was sunk in the waters of the East Indian Ocean. The encounter with a freshwater shark in an African lake is fictional, the result of the sometimes over-romantic imagination of my biographer. Fortunately, my arms were out of the water and so unimpeded by the fluid. I heaved myself up to my waist and drove down with the knife and rammed it at least three inches into the corpse-colored eye. Blood spurted, and the shark raced away so swiftly that it almost tore the knife loose from my hands.

Its tail did curve out enough to scrape across my belly, and my blood was mingling with its blood.

I expected the shark to come back. Even if my knife had pierced that tiny brain, it would be far from dead, and the odor of blood would drive it mad.

It came back as swiftly as a torpedo and as deadly. I dived this time and was enclosed in a distorted world the visible radius of which was a few feet. Out of the distortion something fast as death almost hit me, and went by, and I shoved the knife up into the belly. But the tip only penetrated about an inch, and this time the knife was pulled from my grip. I had to dive for it at once; without it I was helpless. I caught it just before it sank out of reach of eye and hand, and I swam to the surface. I looked both ways and saw a shadow speeding toward me. Then another shadow caught up with it, and blood boiled out in a cloud that hid both sharks. I swam away with as little splash as possible, hoping that other sharks would not be drawn in by the blood and the thrash of the battle.

Before I had gone a half-mile, I saw three fins slicing the water to my left, but they were intent on following their noses to where the blood was flowing, where, as the Yanks say, the action was.

It was a few minutes to twelve P.M. when my plane blew up. About sixteen minutes later, according to my wristwatch, I reached the shore and staggered across the beach to the shade and a hiding place in a bush. The fall, the fight with the shark, and the swimming for a mile at near top speed, had taken some energy from me. I walked past thousands of sea gulls and pelicans and storks, which moved away from me without too much alarm. These would be the great-great-great-grandchildren of the birds that I had known when I was young. The almost completely landlocked lagoon on the beach was no longer there. It had been filled in and covered over years ago by the deposit of sand and dirt from the little river nearby and by the action of the Benguela Current. The original shore, where I had roamed as a boy, was almost two miles inland.

The jungle looked unchanged. No humans had settled down here. Gabon is still one of the least populated countries of Africa.

Inland were the low hills where a broad tongue of the tall closed-canopy equatorial forest had been home for me and The Folk and the myriad animals and insects I knew so well. Most of the jungle in what is now the National Park of the Little Loango is really bush. The rain forest grows only on the highlands many miles inland except for the freakish outthrust of high hill which distinguishes this coastal area.

After resting an hour, I got up and walked inland. I was headed toward the place where the log house of my human parents had once been, where I was born, where the Nine first interfered with my life and started me on that unique road, the highlights of which my biographer has presented in highly romanticized forms.

The jungle here looks like what the civilized person thinks of as jungle, when he thinks of it at all. His idea, of course, is mostly based on those very unrealistic and very bad movies made about me.

Knife in hand, I walked quietly through bush. Even if it wasn't the true jungle of my inland home, I still felt about ten times as happy and at ease as I do in London or even in the comparatively unpopulated, plenty-of-elbow-room environs of my Cumberland estate. The trees and bushes here were noisy with much monkey life, too many insects, and an abundance of snakes, water shrews, mongooses, and small wild cats or long-necked servals. I saw a scale-armored anteating pangolin scuttling ahead of me and glimpsed a tiny furry creature which might or might not have been a so-called "bushbaby." The bird life made the trees colorful and the air raucous. The salt air blowing in from the sea and the sight of the familiar plants made me tingle all over.

As I neared the site of the buildings my father had built eighty-two years ago, I saw that the mangrove swamp to the north had spread out. Its edge was only a quarter of a mile to my left.

I cast around and within a few minutes found the slight mounds which marked the place where I had been born. Once there had been a one-room house of logs and, next to it, a log building just as large, a storehouse. My biographer neglected to mention the store-room, because he ignored details if they did not contribute to the swift development of the story. But, since he did state that an enormous amount of supplies was landed with my parents, it must have been obvious to the reader that the one-room house could not have held more than a fraction of the materials.

Both buildings had fallen into a heap of dead wood and had been covered up by sand and dirt blown by the sea winds and by mud pouring down from the low ridge inland of the buildings. The ridge was no longer there; it had eroded years ago. A bush fire had taken away all the vegetation on it and then the rains had cut it down before new vegetation could grow.

On one side, six feet under the surface, would be four graves, but in this water-soaked, insect-infested soil the decayed bones had been eaten long ago.

I had known what to expect. The last time I'd been here, in 1947, the ravages of fifty-nine years had almost completed the destruction. It was only sentiment that had brought me back here. I may be infra-human in many of my attitudes, but I am still human enough to feel some sentiment toward my birthplace.

I had intended to stand there for a few minutes and think about my dead parents and the other two buried beside them. But mostly about what I had done inside the cabin with the books and the tools I had found in 1898, when I did not know what a book or a tool or a chronological date was, let alone the words for them in English or in any human tongue. And I especially wanted to recreate the day when I had first seen the long ash-blonde hair of Clio Jeanne de Carriol.

There were others with her, of course, and they were the first white-skinned males I had ever seen, outside of the illustrated books I had found in the storehouse. But Clio was a woman, and I was twenty, so my eyes were mainly for her. I did not know nor would have cared that she was the daughter of a retired college teacher. Nor that he had named his daughter Clio after the Muse of History. Nor that they were descended from Huguenots who had fled France after the Revocation of the Edict of Nantes and established plantations and horse farms in Georgia, Virginia, and Maryland. All I knew about the world outside a fifty-mile square area was what I had tried to understand in those books, and most of that I just could not grasp.

I suppose I was lost in thought for a little more than a minute. Then I turned a little to the east, because I'd heard a very faint and unidentifiable noise, and I saw a flash up in a tree about fifty yards away.

I dived into a bush and rolled into a slight depression. The report of the rifle and the bullet striking about ten feet from me came a second later. Three heavy machine guns and a number of automatic rifles raked through the bush. Somebody twenty yards to the north shouted, and a grenade blew up the earth exactly over the site of the storehouse.

I had to get out, and swiftly, but I could not move without being cut down, the fire was so heavy.

Leave it to the Nine to do a thorough job.

They had found out that I was flying a plane from Port-Gentil, ostensibly to Setté Cama. They—their agents, rather—had figured that I might be stopping off at the *Parc National du Petit Loango* for a sentimental pilgrimage. Actually, my main purpose was to leave the plane there and set off on foot across the continent to the mountains in Uganda. It would take me a long time to make the approach to the secret caves of the Nine, but it was better to travel through the jungle across the central part of Africa than to fly anywhere near it. In the jungle, I am silent and unseen, and even the Nine cannot distract me except by accident.

But the Nine had sent that outlaw fighter jet to shoot me out of the sky. And, as a backup for Death, they had arranged an ambush at my birthplace. When the jet pilot had reported in, as he surely must have, that I had gone down with my plane, the Nine had not pulled off their ambushers at once. I suppose they may have had orders to wait there a week. The Nine always were enthusiastic for overkill and overcaution, especially when one of their own—a traitor—was to be taken care of.

Even so, they must have been surprised, they must not have really expected me to come along so soon after being burned to death or smashed flat against the ocean and then eaten by sharks. But they had maintained a very good silence. The wind was blowing from the sea, so I had not heard or smelled them. I think I caught them by surprise; they may not have been sure that I was the one for whom they were waiting.

The grenade was close enough to half-deafen me but I was not confused or immobilized. I rolled away and then crawled toward the men shooting at me. Or shooting where they thought I should be. Gouts of dirt fell over my naked back and on my head. Bushes bent, and leaves fell on me. Another grenade exploded near the first. Bullets screamed off, and pieces of bark fell before me. But I did not believe they could see me. I would have been stitched with lead in a few seconds.

One thing, some of them must have seen that I was only armed with a knife, and that would make them brave.

Suddenly, there was silence except for a man shouting in English. He was telling them to form a ring, to advance slowly to contract the ring, and to fire downward if they saw me. They must not fire into each other. They must shoot at my legs, bring me down, and then finish me off.

If I'd been in his place, I would have done the same. It was an admirable plan and seemed to have a one hundred percent chance of success. I was as disgusted as I had time for. I should have approached more cautiously and scouted the area. I had made the same mistake they did, in essence, except that they were better equipped to rectify theirs.

I kept on going. I did not know how many men they had. I had determined that ten weapons had been firing. But others might be withholding their fire. It would take them some time to form a ring, since they had all been on one side of me. In this thick bush, they would have to proceed slowly and keep locating each other by calling out.

Men circled around swiftly and noisily. I could smell them; there were ten men on that side. So that meant there had to be as many or more ahead of me. Some had been holding back their fire.

I looked upward. I was close to the tree from which the flash had come as a sniper shifted his rifle. He was still about twenty feet up on a branch and waiting for me to make a break for it. I scrutinized the other trees around me for more snipers, but he seemed to be the only one.

I sprang out from under the broad leaves of the elephant's-ear and threw my knife upward. It was a maneuver that had to be done without hesitation and which involved much danger, since it meant I would be revealed, if only for a moment.

It was, however, unexpected. And the only one who saw me before I ducked back under the plant was the sniper. His surprise did not last long. He saw me and the knife about the same time, and then the knife caught him in the throat. The rifle fell out of his hands and onto the top of a bush. He sagged forward but was held from falling by the rope around his waist, tied to the trunk. The knife had made a chunking and the rifle a thrashing as it slid through the branches of the bush. But the shouts of the men had covered it up.

The rifle was a Belgian FN light automatic rifle using the 7.62mm cartridge. It could be set for semi-automatic or automatic fire, and its magazine when full contained twenty rounds. I set it for automatic fire, since I was likely to be needing a hose-like action in thick foliage. It was regrettable that I did not have the knife, but, for the moment, I would have to do without it. I did not want to climb up to the body and so expose myself to fire from below. At any moment one of them might see the corpse and know that I was on the loose with the firearm.

The voices of the men to the east came closer. The ones behind me and on my sides were not closing in so swiftly. One, or more, had grenades, and I especially had to watch out for them.

My heart was pumping hard, and I was quivering with the ecstasy of the hunt. Whether I am the hunter or the hunted, I feel the same. There is a delicious sense of peril; the most precious thing is at stake. You, a living being, may be dead very shortly. And since my life could last forever, or over thirty thousand years anyway, I have much more than most people to lose. But

I didn't think of that. I am as willing to risk it now as I will be thirty millennia from now, if I live that long.

When the nearest man was within ten feet, he had a man on his right about twenty feet away and a man on his left about thirty. He had turned his head to say something to the man behind him. The butt of my rifle drove through the branches of a bush into his throat.

He fell backward and then I was on him and had squeezed his neck with my hands. I took his knife and a full magazine, which I carried clamped under my left arm. But another man about twenty feet behind him had noticed that his predecessor had disappeared.

He spoke in English with an Italian accent. "Hey, Brodie, where are you? You all right?"

I answered back in an imitation of Brodie's voice. "I fell down in this damned bush!"

The man advanced cautiously, then stopped and said, "Stand up so I can see you!"

I put on Brodie's green digger's hat—it was several sizes too small—and rose far enough so he could see the hat and the upper part of my face. He said something and came toward me, and I threw Brodie's knife into his solar plexus.

At the same, there was a yell from behind me. The dead sniper had been discovered.

The leader, bawling out in a Scots English, told everyone to stand still. They were not to start firing in a panic, or they would be killing each other. And they were to call out, in order, identifying themselves.

I waited, and when the time came, I called out with Brodie's voice and then the voice of the Italian. I did not know his name, and the leader could have tripped me up there. But he gave each man's name himself before requiring an answer.

I counted thirty-two men. Some of them were, like the Italian, backing up the enclosers in case I should break loose.

By then I had gotten close enough to the man on my left to cut his jugular vein from behind with the edge of the knife.

It seemed to me that I had an aisle of escape. I could get away and be miles inland, and once I was in the rain forest of the higher lands, I could not be caught.

But I have pride. I wanted to teach the Nine another lesson and also cut down the numbers opposing me. Also, it seemed to me their base must be nearby and that they must have a powerful short-wave transceiver there.

Still, there are times to be discreet, and this was one. I went on into the jungle. I had gotten about fifty yards when I heard muffled shouts. They had discovered the bodies, and they would be scared now. No doubt many, if not all of them, knew who I was. They would have known my abilities in the jungle by report and now they knew by experience. Moreover, adding to the desperation at having me loose would be the desperation at having to report failure to the Nine. They might as well be dead if I escaped.

I tried to figure where the radio would most likely be stationed. At one time, I could have told you, with my eyes shut, exactly where every tree and bush and open area were. But the place had changed too much; I might as well be in completely new territory. Finally, I took to the trees.

I carried the FN strapped over my shoulder, and in the

foliage at the top I removed it. I could see ten of the thirty-one; the others were hidden in the bush. Nine were congregated around a tall thin man with a thick black moustache. His hands flew and his mouth worked as he gave orders.

I had seen him before, and now that I recreated his voice in my mind, I remembered it, too. I had heard it in the caves where the Nine hold their annual ceremonies, where the members of their ancient organization come for the grisly rites they must endure in order to get the elixir of youth. He had not had a moustache then and he had not been wearing clothes and it had been ten years ago, so I did not immediately recognize him.

His name was James Murtagh, a name not too different from his real name or that of his notorious father. He was born in 1881 in Meiringen, Switzerland, but was raised from the age of eight in Wales. Like his father, he was an extremely talented mathematician, if not a genius, and he had taught higher mathematics at Oxford and the University of Talinn. He looked as if he was about forty, so I suppose that it was in 1921 that he was invited by the Nine to join them.

Murtagh had not said a word about himself to me or to anyone that I knew. But the Countess Clara Aekjaer, the beautiful Danish Valkyrie who was my companion during the ceremonies over the years, knew much about him. She told me everything she knew. Perhaps she had been told to do so by the Nine, who were grooming me, without my knowing it, to become one of them if one died.

I could have gotten him with a single shot from my FN, but he might be a link to the next one higher up in the chain. So I set the rifle for automatic and sprayed about twelve rounds into the group. Five fell; the others dived into the bush. I dropped the rifle and slid down the tree before they could get reorganized and blast me from the treetops. I went through the bush southward. It did not seem likely that the base for the group would be in the mangrove swamp to the north.

By then the men were firing at the tree I had left. I continued to travel south while the sound of the weapons grew fainter. Then I heard a voice ahead and, a few minutes later, I peered through a bush at a large clearing. It may have been small a few days before, but axes and powersaws had cut trees and bushes down, and a jeep with a winch had dragged off the fallen plants. There were two large helicopters, Bristol 192's, at one end and six tents near my end. Inside the largest tent was radio equipment on a table; three men were by the equipment. An antenna reached high above the tent.

I scouted around the entire perimeter of the camp and found no hidden guards. I also was alert for booby traps and mines. Murtagh impressed me as the type of man who would think of such devices and smile while he was setting them. I appreciate that, since I also smile when engaged in similar activities.

There was a good chance that Murtagh would send men packing back to the camp. He would figure that I would know a camp had to be close and would go looking for it. He had not set guards around it because he had not really expected that I would survive the attack by the jet. I had to work fast.

Even though much of the vegetation had been dragged away, there were still clumps of uprooted bushes and the stumps of trees in the clearing. I ran bent over across the clearing, approaching the big tent from its closed rear. There I listened to the operator relay orders from his superior officer. Someone in the group that had tried to ambush me had reported via wireless that I had escaped. So the big short-wave set was transmitting a request for two jets and two more helicopters. These would carry napalm bombs and would bring in more men and dogs.

The code name used for me was Tree Lord, which I thought both appropriate and amusing.

I was puzzled about where the jets and copters could be based. It did not seem likely that they would be at Port-Gentil. This was approximately one hundred and twenty-six miles to the northeast. The men in the tent talked as if they expected the craft in about ten minutes. Somewhere, probably in a man-made clearing in the interior, was a base. Had it been set up some time ago just for me? Or was it a multipurpose base? It seemed more probable that it was multipurpose. Otherwise, why had not all its personnel and machines been sent down here to terminate me?

I went around the side of the tent to the opening. Two shots sent the two officers spinning backward and onto the ground. The operator had a .45 automatic in a holster. But he made no motion toward it. He placed his palms flat against the table and stared at me with his mouth open. His huge round eyes, pale skin, shock of wheat-colored hair, sharp beaky nose, and the ear-phones made him look like a very frightened owl.

"Tell them to cancel the operation," I said. "Tell them I've been killed."

He hesitated, and I stepped closer to him. The muzzle of the rifle was only a few inches from his temple. He gulped and obeyed me.

After he had finished, he stared at me as if he expected me to blow his head off. He had a right to expect it, and I had a right to do it, though I have never bothered about rights as defined by human beings unless they happened to coincide with my beliefs. He was a member of an organization devoted to killing me; he knew it and had taken part in it; he deserved to die.

My own philosophy is simple and practical and not at all based on the idea that life is sacred. If a man is out to kill you, you kill him first. This has nothing to do with the rules of warfare as conducted by nations. When I was a member of the British forces in World War II, I observed the Geneva rules. That is, I did except in two cases, where I had orders from the Nine, and their orders superseded anybody's. In return for giving me a very extended youth, they demanded a high price sometimes. But I had had no qualms about killing the men the Nine wanted out of the way, especially since they were the enemy. If I were to tell you that several of them were the highest and most famous of our enemy, you might find it difficult to believe. Especially since the world believes that they committed suicide to keep from falling into the hands of the Russians.

"Do what I say, and quickly, and I'll spare you," I said. "And if you know anything about me, you know I don't go back on my word."

He gulped and nodded. "Can you get Dakar?" I said.

He could do so, and he did at once, asking for Brass Bwana. He was operating illegally, of course, and what the authorities at Dakar thought, I did not know or care. The station was at the time out in the desert about thirty miles from Dakar, had been operating on a mobile basis for twenty-six years, and so far the police had not been able to come near it. I had used it when I worked for the Nine but had never told anyone else in the organization about it. Its operators were criminals, loyal to me, because I had rewarded them well. Now they were in contact with the organization that Doc Caliban had used when he was a disciple of the Nine. This station was somewhere in the Vosges and tied in with another in the Black Forest area of Germany.

I would have preferred to talk directly, but I could not do that and be free to look and listen for Murtagh and his men. The first thing I did was to tell the Dakar people that the code name for me was changed and that I would use the next name on the list the next time I contacted them. I also explained, briefly, that I had been forced to contact them through an enemy. I asked for Doc Caliban, using his code name of Brass Bwana, of course. A minute passed, and then Dakar relayed the message that Caliban could not answer himself. But my message would be passed on to him. However, he had left a message for me.

"The goblin has gone mad, and he is our enemy and the enemy of our enemies his former friends. The goblin is holed up, but we are digging him out."

I thanked Dakar and signed off.

"Do you know German?" I asked the operator.

He said he didn't, but he might have been lying. Not that it mattered. He was not likely to know that the goblin had to be Iwaldi, the old dwarf of the Nine. When I say old, I mean very ancient. He was at least ten thousand years old and possibly thirty thousand. If I understood Caliban's phrasing correctly, Iwaldi had gone insane and turned against the others of the Nine, too. Doc Caliban knew where he was and was going after him. Iwaldi was in the castle of Gramzdorf in the Black Forest. Though Caliban and I had been able to find out very little about any of the Nine's secret hideouts, we had discovered that Iwaldi lived at least part of the year in the castle near the village of Gramzdorf. Caliban had gone there with two of his men, recent recruits who were sons of the men who had been his aides in the old days. The fathers were dead now, but the sons had taken their places beside Doc.

I opened the case of the equipment and smashed the tubes with a hammer and ripped the wires out. Then I cut a slit through the back of the tent and ordered Smith, the operator, to step out ahead of me. We went swiftly to another tent which contained a number of firearms and belts on which to carry grenades. I put about seven grenades in hooks on a belt which I had secured across my chest. I tied Smith's hands behind him and secured him to a bush. It took me a minute to toss a grenade into each of the interiors of the two copters from a distance of two hundred feet. They exploded and burned furiously; they were indeed beautiful, though a little awing. I have never gotten over some feeling of awe for the larger machines that mankind makes. I suppose it's the residue of the first impact of civilization on me. When I blew those two fine but deadly machines, I was asserting the defiance of the savage against the complex and bewildering works of the technological man.

"Where is the base camp?" I asked Smith. "Don't stall. I haven't the time to play around."

"It's about thirty miles northeast of here," he said.

There wasn't time to find out if he was lying or not. I went into the bush by the edge of the camp.

The burning gasoline roared so that I could not hear Murtagh and his men, and the smoke was so intense that I could not have smelled them even if they had been upwind. But I could see quite well, and I smiled as I saw the scared or grim faces peeking from around bushes. They were not about to venture into the camp, since I might be waiting to ambush the ambushers.

Murtagh, of course, would wait until the two copters appeared and then bring them down for protection. But he did not do so. At least, not where I had thought he would. Instead, the men walked away. I had gone around them to come up behind them but by the time I got near the north end of camp, I found them gone. They were easy to track, which I did on a parallel path. It was well that I did, since the canny Murtagh had placed four men at two places to catch me if I came loping along after them. Each couple was back to back to make sure that I did not sneak up on them. I still could have wiped them out with short bursts from my concealment, but I did not see any reason to notify Murtagh that I was on to them. I passed them by and presently was alongside the double file of men heading for the beach. Murtagh was in the lead, and four men who kept watching over their shoulders were the rear guard.

Murtagh was about six feet five and had very rounded shoulders and a forehead that bulged out like the prow of a ship. He removed his hat once to wipe a completely bald pate. The hair that rimmed the back of his head was gray. His eyes were set deeply under a bulging supraorbital ridge. His jaws were so outthrust he might have been an aboriginal Australian. His long neck was bent forward so that he always seemed to be sniffing for something, like a snake. The snakishness was emphasized by the steady movement of his face from side to side.

Behind him was a man carrying a flame-thrower and about six men behind him was another man with a flame-thrower.

I went ahead to a point equidistant from both men and then I fired six bursts. The first shattered the equipment on the back of the first man, but the liquid did not catch fire. The men between the first target and the second went down, and then the flame-thrower on the second man exploded in a globe of fire that enveloped two men behind him.

I was away, rolling down a slight slope and then crawling into its bottom and along it until I reached a shallow ravine. The vegetation and the dirt above me whipped and flew as if a meteor stream had struck it. The firepower poured out in my direction was impressive and must have terrified the birds and the monkeys. But I was not hit.

I made a mistake by not killing Murtagh then. I should not have spared him because of wanting to take him prisoner for questioning later. But I did not regret not having killed him. Though I admit quite readily that I've made a mistake or erred, I never regret. What has been always will be and what is is. And what will be is unknown until the proper time.

Five minutes later, two huge helicopters settled down on the beach. The armed men in them got out and took their stations with the others along the edge of the beach and the jungle. Murtagh got new radio equipment from the helicopters, and the men of the Nine were ready to go into business.

My business was to get out as fast as I could, but I did not do so. I had been running so hard and so long from the Nine that I could not resist the temptation to give them even more punishment. I did, however, retreat to the north and into the swamp. I climbed to the top of a mangrove where I could get a good view. It was well that I did. While the men on the ground stayed on the beach, the two helicopters flew inward and dropped six napalm bombs. Two jets came in and shot six explosive rockets at random within a quarter-mile square area. Then they dropped napalm bombs and returned to strafe the jungle near the burning areas. After their ammunition was exhausted, they flew off, presumably to reload for another trip.

If I had been hanging around close to the men on the beach, I would have been burned to an ash. Still, they had no means of knowing that I was there, and it seemed a very inefficient and expensive method of trying to kill me. Not that the Nine care for expense or for inefficiency if the goal is attained.

With ten baying bloodhounds and six German shepherds, the men on the ground split into two groups. Each went around the burning area. I did not know what garment of mine the dogs could have sniffed at, but I was sure that the Nine had located something in my castle at Grandrith. They weren't likely to pick up any odor from me near the napalmed area, since the smoke would deaden the nerves in their noses. But if they did pick up something near the edge of the swamp, the men would suppose that I was in there, and the mangroves would get a shower of the terrible jellied gasoline. The copters were overhead now, one over each group, waiting for orders.

I climbed down and waded through the brownish, vegetation-sticky waters between the massive buttress-rooted mangroves. After a mile of this, during which I saw several mambas and a large river otter, I went south and came out on dry ground, comparatively dry, that is. Though this was not the rainy season, it was still raining every day, and the soil around here seldom became dry. My footprints would have been evident if I had not been at such pains to walk only on fallen vegetation. Even so, I was leaving a trail which the dogs could pick up easily enough.

As I headed east toward the highlands and the rain forest, I heard the distant whirring of an approaching chopper. It came through the smoke in the distance and then was suddenly headed toward me. It had come at a bad time for me. I was in a natural clearing caused by erosion of the thin soil from a sloping sandstone mass.

The swamp was a quarter-mile to my left. The edge of the clearing on my right was about fifty yards. Ahead was thick bush with about a mile to go before I reached the foot of the cliff which reared up to about five hundred feet. This was the first of the heights which, a few miles inland, became a series of plateaus about five hundred to eighteen hundred feet high and which was covered with the closed-canopy rain forest. This was the tongue of the highlands which extended from the interior and was a freakish formation for this part of the land. Along the coast here, the land was generally flat for about eight to ten miles from the sea to the highlands.

I ran on ahead, glanced back once, and saw two dark objects streaking toward me. I threw myself on the ground, forgetting that I had to be careful not to dislodge the grenades attached to my belt by their pins. The explosions half-deafened me, and dirt showered me. But the rockets had overshot me by forty yards and blown up in a shallow depression. I was up and into the bush ahead and then into the smoke created by the explosions before the wind had a chance to clear it. The next two explosions came behind me. Apparently the rocket man in the chopper had compensated immediately for the overshooting, and if I had stayed in the same place, I would probably have been blown to bits.

As it was, the impact knocked me forward; I felt as if a log had been slapped across my back by a giant. But the impact was softened by the trees and bushes between me and the rockets, and I was up and going again. The smoke from the second volley was carried eastward by the wind and so veiled me from the chopper for a minute.

The huge helicopter came charging through the smoke, its pilot apparently assuming that I was either dead or incapacitated by the explosions. Perhaps he did not release the napalm bombs because he had orders to take me alive if he could do so. Or perhaps he just wanted to make sure he could plant his bombs exactly on the spot where my body or its remnants were and so ensure obliteration of me.

Whatever his reasons, he brought the chopper down to fifty feet above the ground and at a speed of about fifty miles an hour. I was completely at his mercy or seemed to be, because he was suddenly about ten feet to the north of me. The gunners on the right side saw me a few seconds after I saw them, and the snouts of their .50 caliber machine guns began flaming.

They were not, as usual, accurate but they did not need to be, because they were bringing their fire around like water from a hose, and the intersection would be my body.

I did not try to run away, because they had spotted me, and I could not get away when they were that close. I stood up, while the gouts of dirt and pieces of bush torn by the bullets swung toward me. I yanked a grenade from the belt, leaving the pin attached to the belt, and I threw the grenade.

They would have expected me to fire back with my rifle, but this they had never expected. The grenade flew exactly as I had aimed it, went through the open port before the gunner on my right just as the bullets were on the point of intersecting, the scissors of lead about to close on my body.

But the gunner, or someone in the chopper, had been alert and cool enough to catch the grenade and start to throw it out the port. He was not, however, quite swift enough, and the grenade exploded in his hand. The covering of flesh was enough to soften its effect. He was killed and I suppose everybody else in the chopper was, too. But the fuel did not catch fire, not immediately, anyway. The chopper tilted and slid at a forty-five degree angle away from me and into a tree trunk about ten feet above the ground. By then I was running, and when I saw a gully, I dived into it. I was flying through the air when the fuel and napalm did go off, and I felt the heat pass over the gully. My bare back was almost seared.

My face was turned away, and I was breathing shallowly, because I did not want to sear my lungs. Then I was up and out, because if the first blast had not gotten me, I had a chance to get away.

The heat felt as if it were scorching the hairs off my legs and the back of my head, and smoke curled around me. But the explosion had taken place about a hundred and fifty yards away, and the heavy bush helped screen me. The napalm bombs were not large ones.

The other copter had hung back for some reason or other. Perhaps it was attached to the men with the dogs and was to play a part if the dogs treed me. But when the first chopper exploded, the second came up swiftly enough. It, however, stayed about three hundred feet up as its crew observed the wreck. They had no idea whether the copter had crashed accidentally or whether I had brought it down with my firearm.

I remained under the thick elephant's-ear plant. An observer in the air can see much more than one on the ground in these conditions. Heavy as the bush was, it still had open spaces across which I had to cross, however briefly, and once I was seen I had little chance to get away.

The chopper did not hover long over the wreck. It began to swing in a wide circle around, apparently hoping to flush me out or catch sight of me. Then it went back west, and I left my hiding place and traveled swiftly eastward. Just before I reached the bottom of the first cliff, I had to conceal myself again. The chopper was returning. It went by about a hundred feet above me and two hundred yards to the north. It contained a number of men and dogs.

I could not see it, but I guessed that it had settled down on the edge of the cliff and that dogs and men were getting out of it. Their plans now were to push me east with one party and hope to catch me with the one now ahead. Then I was able to see the faces of some men as they watched from the lip of the cliff. The copter took off again and began circling around. Occasionally, the machine guns in it spat fire. I could not hear the guns above the roar of the copter, but some of the bullets struck close enough for me to hear their impact against the trees. They were probing in the hope they could scare me out.

If I stayed where I was, the dogs of the party behind me might pick up my scent. Their baying and barking was getting closer. It was difficult to determine in that muffling foliage, but it seemed that they were headed straight toward me.

I was beginning to feel that I had gone through enough for one day. To survive a twelve hundred foot fall into the ocean and a shark attack should be enough excitement for a month, anyway, not to mention blowing up two helicopters on the ground and lobbing a grenade into the port of another in the air. And getting through the firepower of thirty-five men and a rocket-carrying, napalm-bomb-dropping aircraft. I had had enough for some time; surely my luck must be running out. My anger was getting dangerous, dangerous for me, that is. I could not afford to lose control. But I was feeling a tiredness very new to me. Those who have read the volumes by my biographer, or Volume IX of my own memoirs, know that my energy is great. It can be called animal-like. But I had gone through an experience only two months ago which might be called unmanning. Afterward, I had had to go into hiding from the Nine with my wife and Doc Caliban and his cousin, Trish Wilde. I had been without adequate sleep for a week. I wanted to get back to the rain forest of my childhood and youth, to see the dark ceiling close over me, to hear the silence and feel the coolness of the green womb.

I crouched under the bush and tried to suppress my trembling. I bit my lips and clutched the rifle as if I could squeeze in the stock with my fingers. I wanted to leap up and run toward the enemy with my gun blazing and, when that was empty, throw my grenades, and when those were gone, close in on them with the knife.

The images were vivid and satisfying, but they were deadly. I enjoyed them, then laughed to myself, and some of the shaking went away. I had to get out from the closing jaws by going north to the mangrove swamp or south through more bush. Men were already descending from the cliff on both sides and five dogs were with each column. Their ascent was slow and dangerous, but they were determined to extend the jaws of the trap. Other men stayed on top of the cliff to observe. And the dogs were getting closer now; I could hear them plainly because the chopper had traveled to my south. And then it rose and two objects fell from it, and the jungle to my right was a hemisphere of flame and a spire of inky smoke.

The chopper swung back and over me, past me, stopped high above the edge of the swamp, and two more bombs fell. The mangroves for a stretch of a hundred yards were burning fiercely.

Their plan was a good one. Of course, they did not know I was surrounded, but they were acting as if I were. And, as sometimes happens, the *as-if* hypothesis was going to bear a theory and then a fact. Unless I managed, like many a hard fact, to slip through the net of hypothesis.

There was only one thing to do. I crawled toward the left and into the edge of the smoke cloud. Though I was as close to the ground as I could get, I could not stay there long without coughing. Nor could I depend on the smoke to conceal me because of the vagaries of the wind. My purpose was to get where the dogs coming down from the cliff could not smell me or to get as close as possible to that area. Also, when I left that area, I would be reeking of smoke, which I hoped would cover up my body odor.

A man was saying something to a bloodhound, and then they were past me. I came up behind him, crouching, and broke his neck by twisting his head. Before he had fallen to the ground, I had also broken the neck of the dog. All this took place within twelve feet of the closest man and dog, but the roaring of the flames and the smoke swirling through the thick bush hid the noise and the sight of the dead. It took me a minute to get the dead man's clothes off and onto me. They fitted fairly well, since he was almost my height, six feet three inches, and he had a large frame.

The green digger's hat and the green shirt enabled me to get close to another man who did not have a dog, and he went down with a knife in his neck before he realized that I was the hunted. The next two victims were another man and a dog. I almost got caught, because a man was about ten paces behind them, but the bush concealed us long enough for me to be ready by the time he stumbled across the bodies.

They should have stayed back and let the helicopter saturate the area with napalm. They would have gotten me. But as long as they made the mistake of trying to roust me out with men and dogs in a bush in which I had lived a good part of my eighty-one years, they were bound to suffer. I then walked up the cliff, limping as if I'd hurt myself. I looked up twice and saw several men looking at me, and one was shouting at me, if his wide open and writhing mouth meant anything. I continued to limp and several times sat down as if I'd been badly hurt.

Halfway up the cliff, I saw two men coming down toward me. Apparently they were sent by their officer to find out if I had been wounded by their quarry. I sat down with my back to the descending men. The copter was circling tightly about two hundred yards away almost on a level with me. I could see some men and dogs two hundred feet below as they passed from bush to bush, but most of the enemy were concealed. Two men were coming toward me, and three men were on top of the cliff. I had to act swiftly.

My try at passing myself off as one of them failed. A man called down to me, "Cramer?" evidently thinking I must be the man whose clothes I'd taken. One look at my face would tell him his mistake.

I got up onto my legs as if it was painful to do so, with my face still turned away. The rifle was hanging from a strap over my shoulder, and my hands were empty, so that that must have lowered their guard, if indeed it was up at all.

"What the hell, Cramer," the man said in English with a Hungarian accent. "You know better than to leave your station! Did that wild man get you or did you just fall down, trip over your own feet, you clumsy lout?"

"Neither!" I said, and whirled around, the knife coming out of its sheath and through the air and into the Hungarian's solar plexus. The other man froze just long enough for me to pull the automatic from its open holster and shoot him in the chest.

Then I continued to fire up at the three faces hanging over the cliff's edge, three white faces with black O's of mouths. The Luger was a .45, the range was two hundred feet and at a difficult angle and at small targets, so I missed. I had expected this, but the faces did disappear, and I threw the automatic down, withdrew the knife and stuck it in its sheath, and ran up the steep and treacherous path—fit only for goat or baboons—removing my rifle as I did. A glance at the copter showed that, so far, the men in it had not noticed me. They were intent on something below them.

That would not last long. The men on top of the cliff had to have a transceiver of some sort, and they would notify the copter immediately.

By then, the top of the cliff was about one hundred and sixty feet away. I stopped, yanked out another grenade, and cast it. The grenade had to travel about fifty-five feet beyond the range most men can throw a standard hand grenade. It sailed just over the lip of the cliff as the three stuck their heads over to fire at me. The explosion threw rocks and dirt over me, but I saw one body sailing out of the smoke to crash against a projection, roll over and fall the rest of the way. I had to presume that the other two were out of the combat; if I was wrong, I would be dead. The copter had started to whirl around just before I threw the grenade. The pilot must have received the message from the man on the top of the cliff. I was ready for this, I'd yanked out another grenade, and I threw it.

It was probably the best throw of my life, as far as both distance and accuracy went. The grenade weighed about one and three-quarter pounds and the copter was about two hundred feet away when I threw the grenade. It had started to move before then and was coming swiftly. It was approaching nose first, so that its machine gunners could not aim at me. Its rockets had been launched during the first attack, otherwise it could have fired at point-blank range and disintegrated me and a good part of the face of the cliff.

But the pilot must have been jarred by the unexpected blast of the grenade, and he did not react to my pointing my rifle at him because I did not point it. Otherwise, I suppose he would have swung around so that the gunners on one side or the other could let loose.

By the time he decided to do that, the grenade was well launched, and just as he pivoted his craft around and stopped it, the grenade struck the vanes. The vanes and the body of the machine disappeared in a cloud of smoke, pieces of machinery came flying out, the machine dropped almost straight down and crashed. A second later, it was burning furiously, and it may have fallen on a number of men and the exploding fuel may have splashed on some. The men on the ground were shaken up; the fire directed at me as I raced on up the path was ragged and misdirected.

And then I was on top of the cliff, ready to fire at any survivors of the grenade I'd tossed up there. But there were none.

One of the corpses had six grenades attached to hooks on a belt. I tossed these, one at a time, into the bush below the cliff and had the satisfaction of knowing that I got at least two men and a dog. Then I picked up a rifle and left running because I did not want to be there if more copters were called in or if jets were used. As it was, I had just entered a thick bush on top of the next higher plateau when two jets screamed overhead about five hundred feet.

I kept on going and did not stop until I had reached the green cliff of seemingly impenetrable jungle that marks the border of the rain forest. I wormed my way through it and then it was as if I had stepped into a quiet twilight cathedral grown by God. I was home.

And now is as good a place as any to recapitulate the events leading up to those in this volume.

My name is known wherever books and movies are known, and that covers at least three-fourths of the habitable world. Even those who have never read the books or seen the movies know, in a general sense, what my name stands for. (When I say my name I mean the one that my biographer gave me to conceal my real identity.)

My biographer has stretched the truth, added things which never existed, and ignored others that did exist. But, in the main, the first two volumes of my life were based on reality, and the later ones at least springboarded from an actual event. My biographer did give a fairly accurate picture of my personality. Perhaps I should say he reported my basic attitudes, with much verisimilitude, though he softened some of these because he wanted reader identification with me. And he did not go into any depth about the infrahumanity of my thinking. (Although here I may not be fair with him. The creatures who raised me, The Folk, were subhuman, but they did have a language, and I wonder if anybody who uses a language can escape being classified as entirely human. I suppose the dolphins could, since they live in water and lack hands. But The Folk were anthropoids, probably a giant variety of the ancient hominids, Zinjanthropus or Paranthropus. And while their language reflected a very peculiar way of looking at the universe—to English speakers—it was no more peculiar than Shawnee would be to an Englishman. And in many ways their *Weltanschauung* was remarkably close to that of Sunset Strip inhabitants.)

In 1948, I decided to write my memoirs. I could not publish them because I was then serving the Nine, and they wanted no slightest word of their existence printed. Or even spoken of among the noncognoscenti. I could not have published the memoirs if I had omitted any reference to them. Certain obvious phenomena, such as looking as if I were only thirty when I had to be sixty, and the source of my enormous wealth (on a small fraction of which I paid income tax), could not be overlooked by the public or the authorities. Moreover, aside from all this, my statement that I was not a figment of a fiction writer's feverish brain would have resulted in enormous publicity and invasion of my privacy. Not to mention the possibility that I might have been certified.

Nevertheless, I started to write the memoirs. Some day they might be publishable. Also, I liked the idea of remembrance of things past. (Yes, I have read Proust and in French, my favorite human language.) I have an almost photographic memory but it sometimes results in pictures which startle the humans who lived through the same events. Volume I begins with the first day I can remember, when I was suckling and looking up into those beautiful rusty-brown eyes, into the eyes of the only being who loved me for eighteen years. Volume I ends at the age of ten, or what I calculate as the age of ten, the night I first used a knife. Volumes I through VIII covered seventy-eight years. Some of the manuscripts were slim, some were over a million words long. They corrected a number of distortions or omissions of events and told the true names behind the names my biographer used. They included many items of information which I suppose would repulse the readers of my "biography." I have never had any hesitation about eating human meat when the occasion demanded, contrary to what my biographer stated. Nor have I been rigorously Victorian in some aspects of my life, to say the least. And I suppose, in fact, I know, that many would condemn me for serving the Nine. They would equate this with Faustus' selling of his soul.

It is easy enough to scorn. Let the scorner be offered thirty thousand years or more of youth and then we shall hear what they have to say.

My wife and I took the oath under conditions that would make a Mau-Mau initiation look like a Sunday-School Bible presentation. And I suppose we weren't honest or ethical even then, because we had unstated reservations. But we would remain with the Nine, and take their immortality, as long as we were not asked to do anything we just could not do and still respect ourselves. Fortunately, neither of us was asked, though I must admit that I am capable of much that would revolt most of the so-called civilized peoples. But then I have never really considered myself as part of humanity. This attitude can be for bad or good, depending on the circumstances.

Nevertheless, immortality brings a high price. It is true that you pay for everything valuable you get in this world. Nothing is really free. And so, for years, both Clio and myself felt a little less than "clean." That is the only word I can think of that is anywhere appropriate. Thirty thousand or more years ago, some Old Stone Age peoples discovered something that gave them an extremely extended youth. It also made them immune to any disease or to breakdown of the cells. Of course, they could fall down and break their necks or slit their throats or get clubbed to death. But if chance worked well for them, they could live for what must have seemed forever. They did age, but so slowly that a man who took the elixir at the age of twenty-five would only look fifty at the end of fifteen thousand years.

I don't know the history of what happened between 25,000 B.C. and 1913 when the agent of the Nine first introduced himself. By then, the Nine consisted of Anana, a thirty-millennia old Caucasian woman, XauXaz, Ing, Iwaldi, a dwarf, a Hebrew born about 3 B.C., an ancient proto-Bantu, two proto-Mongolians, and an Amerindian. They lived most of the year in various parts of the world, but once a year they held a ceremony which must have originated in the early part of the Paleolithic. This involved the giving up of flesh on the part of the servants of the Nine—a painful procedure—and the drinking of the elixir. The ceremonies were always held in a complex of caves in the remote mountains near Uganda.

Over a period of several months, the "candidates" drank the rejuvenation liquid. No samples were ever given out; the candidates entered the caverns naked and left naked. It meant a hideous death to be discovered trying to smuggle the stuff out.

We "candidates," I estimate, numbered about five hundred. We were the elite of the organization that, literally, ruled the world in secret. How many were enlisted in the lower echelons, I couldn't even begin to guess. The lower echelon, the "servants of the Nine," probably numbered half a million. None of these even knew of the elixir or had ever seen the Nine.

We candidates were those who might be chosen to replace one of the Nine if he or she died.

Volume IX of my memoirs opens with Clio in our estate at Grandrith, which includes a manor, a castle, a forest, and the village of Cloamby. (John Cloamby, Viscount Grandrith, is my true name and title.) I was in our house on the plantation in western Kenya. I was blasted out of my bed by a shell from a Kenyan Army artillery unit because old Jomo Kenyatta had given the order to wipe me off the face of the Earth. I had refused to become a Kenyan citizen or to leave Kenya, and he had put up with this for several years. Then he had decided to kill me (or perhaps somebody else in the Kenyan administration had). I survived and I escaped with the army on my tail. Not only that, an Albanian by the name of Enver Noli was after me with a band of heavily armed Arab bandits. He was hoping that I would lead him to the site of my gold mine in Uganda. I did, though the gold had long been gone. In the meantime, some mysterious enemy had let loose a lion on me. I found out that he was Doc Caliban, accompanied by two aged men, the last survivors of the band that had once helped him in his fight against evil.

Doc Caliban was as strange a phenomenon as I. You might say I was the Feral Man, the Man of the Jungle, whereas Doctor Caliban was the Civilized Man, the Man of the Metropolis. He had been trained since an early age to develop to the fullest potentiality his physical and mental powers, which must have been considerable. In fact, they were probably, next to mine, the greatest. And no wonder, when you consider that our grandfather had been an Early Stone Age Man, XauXaz, the ancient who was second only to Anana in age and power at the round oaken table of the Nine. That was why my bones and Caliban's were so much thicker than modern man's, thus affording a broader base for the attachment of massive muscles.

But we did not know, at the time, that XauXaz was our ancestor.

Caliban was out to kill me because he thought I had killed

his beautiful cousin, Patricia, when she was on a scientific expedition in East Africa.

Both of us were suffering the peculiar and unpredictable side effects of the immortality elixir. Ours occurred about the same time with the result that we each had very strange, and similar, psycho-neuroses. Those who are curious may read Volume IX of my memoirs.

Our first face-to-face encounter came on the natural bridge that leads to the caverns of the Nine. But the Nine stopped us from fighting. XauXaz had died, and we two had been picked out of the five hundred candidates to vie for his place. After the ceremony, we would be set free and one should kill the other.

It was then that Anana told us that we were half-brothers. Our father had also been a candidate, and the elixir had had an unfortunate side effect on him. Lord Grandrith had gone mad. He had, in fact, become that savage maniac known in history as Jack the Ripper.

But he had recovered and he had emigrated to the States, where he took the name of Caliban. The side effects had passed, but they left a consciousness of what he had done and a revulsion against himself. He swore to raise his son to fight evil. I think that he meant eventually to reveal his past to his American son and to turn him against the Nine. He did most of this in secret, and thus, though his child could have established athletic records that would still not be beaten (if I had also abstained), he never entered sports in high school or college.

He did become the greatest surgeon in the world and he also was clearly the greatest in many fields: archeology, chemistry, and a number of other sciences and professions. But he avoided publicity as much as possible. However, a writer found out something about him and used him and his band of aides as the basis for a semifictional series in a pulp magazine. Caliban's "biographies" deviated even more from reality than mine, yet many of the adventures did contain a kernel of truth.

I left the caves and went to a tree house I'd built in the rain forest wherein Clio and I had vacationed. I discovered a madman aping me. He it was who had abducted Trish Wilde, Doc Caliban's cousin. I rescued her, and we went on to England, where I knew that Enver Noli and Doc Caliban were going. Both were intent on getting hold of Clio and using her against me.

By then I was beginning to wonder if the whole situation had not been brought about by the Nine. They could have given both of us something to bring on the "side effects." They could have set up the abduction and supposed death of Trish to cause Caliban to want revenge. And I was sure that the mysterious death of our father was caused by the Nine. They must have discovered that he intended to turn against them and killed him. But his American son, Doc Caliban, did not know anything at all about the Nine and never suspected, until then, that the Nine were responsible. When they offered him immortality, he accepted it, just as I had. Just as, I am convinced, any human would.

At the estate, Caliban and I had killed off Noli's group and then we fought, though I tried to talk him out of it. We tore each other up like two leopard males at mating time, and we both almost died. But one of the properties of the elixir is the regeneration of organs, and we grew our lost ones back.

We also had recovered from the madness brought on by the side effect. We found out we had been duped, and we swore to fight against the Nine. We knew what little chance we had of ever winning. But I killed the men sent to summon us to a meeting of the Nine in London, and we fled.

All this is told in Volume IX of my memoirs.

Since then, Clio and I had been separated from Doc Caliban and his cousin. We had been around the world twice. During the first trip, I had dropped off the manuscript of Volume IX in a Los Angeles post office for your editor to publish. I had met him in Kansas City at the home of a common friend.

We went from Los Angeles to New York. Clio and I made an unchartered flight across the Atlantic in one of Doc Caliban's planes, which we got from a hangar near the tip of Long Island. We flew the jet all the way about twenty feet above the waves. We landed on an unattended strip in Devonshire on land owned by me, and we motored to London. I got in touch with Doc Caliban via the short-wave in our hideout in the apartment in Marylebone Borough. Doc reported that he now had two "sidekicks," sons of two of his former associates. The three men were on the trail of Iwaldi in Germany. He wanted me to come to Germany to join in the hunt, but I told him of my plans to scout out the caves of the Nine. I did not intend to attack anybody there, unless the chance of risk was slight enough to warrant it. I just wanted to map the area in my mind for the day when Doc and I would invade it.

I doubted very much that any of the Nine would be in the caves, since this was not the time for the ceremonies. But I did not know that. I suspected that there would be a formidable army of guards and that the entrances would be mined and booby-trapped. I did not know this, of course, but it seemed unlikely that the caves would be left unguarded. Though they were in a remote and arid mountain range, and the caves could be reached only with difficulty, there were bound to be gold or oil prospectors around there. The Nine had deliberately created a superstitious dread of the area among the natives just outside the mountains. And the Nine doubtless controlled in secret many of those high in the administration of Uganda and Kenya. These would take steps to declare the area officially off limits if the Nine had to kill so many that people got curious.

My plan was to approach the mountains from the west coast of Africa, on foot and alone. If I sailed or flew into the east coast, I might be spotted, and the skein of the Nine would be flung everywhere to catch me. Besides, too many people in Kenya and Uganda knew me. But if I landed quietly on the coast of Gabon and traveled as I like best to travel, alone and lightly armed, I could traverse the rain forests which stretch across much of central Africa. I would avoid all humanity, and I would come like a shadow out of the west. Nobody would expect me. And I should be comparatively free to investigate. It was the western end of the caves that I knew nothing about. All candidates had always been required to follow a strictly limited route from the east, and exploration of the area had been forbidden with a very painful existence and eventually death promised for those who broke the law.

Doc Caliban did not argue with me. He is very self-sufficient. Also, though I could be wrong, I think he preferred not to work with me. He was probably right, since we both are so strongly individualistic. It is not that we can't take orders, because he served with distinction as a commissioned officer in the U.S. Army in 1918. And I was a major and then a colonel in the RAF in World War II. And both of us were under the strictest sort of discipline from ourselves and others when we went through medical school.

But we each have our own way of doing things, and there was in both of us a residue of doubt about who was the strongest. This seems childish, and perhaps is, but after you have *known* for many years that you are the most athletic man alive, the swiftest, the strongest, and then you run across somebody who seems to be fully as strong, then you doubt. Doc and I had fought at Grandrith Castle, and you may read the results of that fight in Volume IX of my memoirs. But when two are so evenly matched, and one wins, the loser is entitled to wonder if the outcome would be different the next time. I'm sure that Doc thought about this at times, chided himself for his juvenility, and then could not keep from speculating again.

So it was best that we tackle the Nine separately, for the time being, anyway.

Clio objected to being left behind, but I did not want to be burdened when I traveled through the rain forest. Tough and strong as this delicate and beautiful little blonde is, she was not born in Africa nor raised ferally. The only human being whom I would have considered taking with me, because he could keep up with me under the primitive conditions, would be Doc Caliban.

So I kissed her goodbye and left London, which I hate because of the crowds and the noise and odors, and flew illegally to various ports. But I made a stop near Port-Gentil to check on some of my operatives, and it must have been there that the agents of the Nine detected me.

I had escaped where I had no right to by the usual mechanism and rules of probability of the universe. But, as I have said, I am convinced that I do have something about me that twists and distorts the odds against coincidence and good luck. It's what I call the "human magnetic moment," and it is what very few people possess. I am one, and Doc Caliban, from what he had told me, must be another. Of course, one day, the inevitable must happen. A bullet will plow into my brain or I'll fall off a tree or down the stairs or an automobile going through a stop sign will crush me or a faulty gas heater will asphyxiate me or... I remember a line from Merrill Moore's poem, "Warning To One": *Death is the strongest of all living things.*

It will come to me as to every man. But until the moment, I will live as if *I* were the strongest of all living things.

I was home again, and I breathed relief, though I knew it might not last long. For the first time in a long time, I could genuinely *breathe.* The air inside the closed-canopy tall equatorial forest is like that nowhere else. It sighs with the greenness of totally alive beings, animals or plants. Contrary to what most people think, this type of rain forest is not hot, even if it is on the equator. It may be staggeringly blistering just above the top of the forest. But below, where the ground is at the bottom of a deep well, roofed over by a tangle of layers and layers of branches and vines and lianas and leaves, it is cool. And the temperature does not vary much. Moreover, the area between the broad and tall trees is often park-like. It is free of that thick mass that can be penetrated only with difficulty by man and that people associate with the word *jungle* because of Hollywood's projections of what it thinks a jungle looks like.

In fact, if Murtagh's forces had caught me on the ground here, they could have blown me apart a dozen times before I fell. The area is too open for the sort of warfare through which I had just gone. Of course, if I had had a chance to get up a tree and into the various levels of the tanglery overhead, I might have gotten away. Here, despite my two hundred and fifty pounds, I could travel from tree to tree for long distances. It wouldn't be by swinging from lianas. That is another Hollywood idea and utterly unrealistic. (Though I have done it several times under extreme emergency conditions.) On foot, and traveling not too swiftly, I have often gone for miles in this area without once setting foot on the ground. And when I was much younger and lighter, I could do it much more swiftly.

Now I stayed on the ground because I wanted to make speed. I trotted along until I found a small pool and drank from it. Then, feeling hungry, I hunted, and I finally saw a small half-grown tusker. I ran after him, and he took off speedily, but I am faster and have more endurance, and eventually he stopped, breathing hoarsely, facing me, his little eyes savage and desperate, saliva dripping from his tusks. I did not use my rifle because of the noise. I sprang in, he tried to wheel to one side, and my knife cut open his jugular. I drank the blood while it was still pumping out and then I butchered the beast. I ate him raw and then proceeded on my way with about half of him— the best half—wrapped up in his hide. There had to be water near, since the bushpig seldom strays too far from water. Then I remembered the small stream about a mile to the north and made for it. I drank and then ate some more of the pig. I was lucky in running across this creature, since they usually lie up in dense reed beds or tall grass by day and come out at night to feed. And they usually run in groups of twenty or so.

I have heard people who did not know that they were talking to me, scoff at my ability to survive in this area. They say that if I had eaten all that raw meat, I would have been infested with worms and other internal parasites.

They overlook that there are any number of natives who eat raw meat from which some get infested and some do not. However, it is my opinion that I never got sick because, one, I lived in a healthy area, the closed-canopy forest, and, two, far more significant, I probably had something in me which killed off all bacteria, viri, and parasites. I am convinced the Nine were dictating the course of my life before birth. I believe that I was injected with something which made me immune, just as I believe that the Nine deliberately set things up so that I was raised as a feral human by The Folk. (The factors which made me conclude this are detailed in Volume II of my memoirs, unpublished as yet.) Thus, my unique way of life was not entirely "natural," any more than Doc Caliban's was natural. This had made me wonder how many other men, known or unknown to history, have been "modified" by the Nine. How many geniuses owe their shaping to the grim ancients who pull the strings from their secret mansions?

I was walking along, noting that it was now twilight at ground level, which meant that the sun must be sinking close to the horizon. It was still comparatively quiet here, though some males of a troop of sooty mangabeys were occasionally giving their loud chattering cry. These were large long-tailed monkeys with gray fur especially long on the sides of the head and with pink faces speckled with gray-brown freckles. They make good eating, as I well know.

I was thinking about going up and making a nest in the middle level when I heard the baying of dogs behind me.

Doctor Murtagh had not given up. I don't know how he had managed to catch up, since I had traveled faster than ordinary men with dogs could, unless he called in more copters.

I dropped the hog, ran to the stream, which was a quarter of a mile away, and washed myself in it. Then I climbed a one hundred and fifty foot high tree to the middle level. From there, I made my way across the tanglery to the source of the baying. I knew that they would find where I had gone up, and they would likely fire into the close-canopy around there. They would be shooting for some distance eastward from where I had ascended on the theory that I was fleeing via the middle level. They would never, I hoped, believe that I had the guts to cross above them and travel behind them.

In about fifteen minutes, I stopped my cautiously slow travel. I hugged a branch which was almost entirely enclosed in lianas and vines and broad leaves. Down on the ground, it was so dark that the men were using flashlights and lamps. Where I was, the sunlight was still filtering down. By looking up, they could have seen me outlined against the lighter sky if it had not been for the dense green around me. My cloak of invisibility. Of course, I could not move now unless I did so very slowly, because my weight would bend the bridge of vegetation between the trees and the noise could be heard by the dogs or even by the less keen ears of the men. However, I could move while they were on the march as long as I trailed them by several hundred yards. They kept on my scent until the dogs broke into an eager baying and barking when they came onto the place where I had killed the bushpig. The dogs went swiftly after that, with the men stabbing their beams on every side. They would have liked to have camped for the night, I'm sure. They were in the territory, and they must have been spooked because of the day's events. But they drove on with Doctor Murtagh at their head and did not stop until they came to the tree up which I had climbed. A moment later, the gunfire that was aimed at the canopy aroused the monkeys and birds for miles around. The screeching continued long after Murtagh had given the cease-fire order.

If I had been hiding overhead anywhere within a hundred-yard square area, I would have been shot a dozen times. As it was, a number of bursts came my way, and I was two hundred yards back and behind a thick trunk. Then they probed the area with flashlights, hoping to find my corpse hanging from a tangle or fallen onto the ground.

Murtagh said nothing when his men reported no success. But his bearing, outlined in the flashlight, was a curse. He gave an order (which I could not hear at that distance, of course) and they pitched camp.

It did not take long. Every man except Murtagh carried a pack on his back. These consisted mainly of ammunition, food, water, medicine, and collapsible furniture and tents.

The tents were Doc Caliban's invention and known only to the servants of the Nine. The tents and the furniture could be likened only to that pocket-sized collapsible sailing ship of Norse mythology, *Skidbladnir*. A man would remove a neatly folded bundle of cloth about the size of a big handkerchief and snap it like a whip. Yards of green material unfolded, shot out like a flag in a breeze. The stuff was as thin and as light as spider webs, but it kept out light and cold, and it was as tough as an inch-thick sheet of aluminum. The framework of the supports for the tent slid out of a cylinder about two feet long and three inches thick and was set up within sixty seconds. Then the material of the tent was arranged over it and tied down at the ends to stakes driven into the thin forest soil. There wasn't much dead wood available for fires, but they did not care. They carried small metal boxes which unfolded and projected six large round rings at the ends of thin metal stalks. These burned a gas derived from a compressed liquid and furnished a fire for cooking or heating. Caliban had invented both the tents and the burners in 1937, but only the Nine had benefited from it then. Many of the things he invented in the 30's are still ahead of their time.

The lamps were set up to bathe the camp with additional illumination. Wires were strung and little buttons were stuck here and there outside and above the camp. The buttons would set off alarms in the camp through the wireless. They were set to react to any mass larger than a monkey which would get near the magnetic field they were radiating.

The tents were arranged in a circle with Murtagh's in the center. There were about fifty men and thirty dogs—enough evidence that copters had brought in additional forces. Double guards were stationed every forty feet outside the perimeter of the line formed by the tents. The area outside was bathed in a bright light, and the guards were relieved every hour. Of course, I could have dropped onto Murtagh's tent, but I didn't relish the idea of falling a hundred feet even after having survived a twelve hundred foot fall that morning. Also, what was the use of killing Murtagh if I got shot to pieces?

For the same reason, I did not shoot him at a distance with my rifle. I had been extremely fortunate to have survived the concentrated fire in the bush. Here, where I had to travel slowly in the canopy, they could have overhauled me and gotten below me unless I was very lucky again. I did not want to stretch my good fortune too far.

I did want to hear what they were saying. Slowly, I crawled through the canopy. This was necessary not only to prevent noise but to test the stuff holding me up. It is not always anchored securely. I have fallen several times when I was a youth living in this area, twice saving myself by hanging onto a liana that did not break and once managing to grab the end of a branch as I fell toward the ground a hundred feet below. I have seen three of The Folk who were not so fortunate when they went through the green trapdoor; they broke most of their bones.

Every now and then the bright beam of a small searchlight fingered the tanglery where I was. The beam was being moved at random; it pierced the forest at ground level, lighting up the huge trunks of the trees, making them look like crudely carved pillars of a deep mine worked by gnomes. And then it would leap up onto the dark ceiling overhead, sometimes catching red in the eyes of the owls and bushbabies and servals.

The men not on guard were eating the food they had cooked in their cans over the gas fires. Murtagh sat on a folding chair by a folding table just inside his tent with several of his officers. When I was directly overhead, I could hear a few words, but most of the conversation in the leader's tent was lost. It would have been convenient if the tent had been under a tree with limbs sticking out only about twenty-five feet above.

Nevertheless, I lay flat on a net of lianas and leaves supported by a thin branch and stared down through the net at the camp. Some of the men had loud voices, and I hoped to learn from them. Two, a French Canadian and a mulatto Congolese, spoke in French, presumably on the theory that Murtagh couldn't understand them. Perhaps he didn't, but I think that an educated and cosmopolitan man such as Murtagh would have been very fluent in this tongue. Perhaps they were depending on him not to comprehend their two types of French. They may have been correct in their assumptions. The Canadian's French was only half-understood by me, and I doubt that a man skilled in Parisian French would understand the Congolese's patois. The two had to repeat much to make their own words clear.

The Congolese said, "If it is true that this white devil's plane was blown up, and he fell a thousand feet without a parachute, and swam ashore and then he got through us and killed half of us... then what are we doing here?"

"We are here because Murtagh said so, and because he is paying us very well," the Canadian said. "That *white* devil as you call him, is insane. He would have to be to take the chances he did. As for his falling that far from a plane, I do not believe that. And..."

"But I heard the report over the radio. I was standing behind Murtagh when the pilot reported. He said the plane exploded, and he saw Grandrith's body falling. He watched it until it disappeared, and there was no parachute."

"I read once about a man who fell two thousand feet into a snowbank and lived," the Canadian said. "It was a true story. It had to be, it was in the French edition of *The Reader's Digest*. It happened during World War II. And I heard about a man who fell a thousand feet into the sea and lived. So, why shouldn't this man live if others can?"

"And how do you explain that he also survived us?" the Congolese said. "Does a man have that much luck, to live through a fall like that and through our firepower and then burn four helicopters and kill fifteen men on the ground? Some with a knife while many others were only ten feet away? And kill dogs, too?"

While they were talking, moonlight fell on me. I was in the lower level of canopy, and above me was an opening in the upper level. I was not, of course, visible to those below me.

I listened carefully. The two discussed Murtagh and their officers and what they would do with their money when they returned to civilization. Then they said a few words about the base, which was apparently to the northeast somewhere, not too far away. The radio operator, Smith, had not lied.

I should have left then. The base was my next goal; I wanted to investigate that and perhaps harass its occupants. I could at least prowl around and pick up information by eavesdropping. Or perhaps abduct someone who might have valuable information which he would give, willingly or not.

But I stayed, hoping I would find out more. And then I heard a thrashing in the leaves behind me and turned swiftly, my knife ready. My rifle and belt with the grenades attached was stretched across a web of lianas. I saw a blurry form in the moonlight—a little guenon monkey, I think it was—and then a larger winged form after it. An eagle-owl had spiraled down through the opening in the upper canopy and spotted a tiny monkey and the monkey had seen it coming. It flashed across a liana and then was on me. I batted at it, struck it to one side; it gave a cry and clutched a twig and then was off, somewhere. I don't know where or care. The owl had been following it so closely that it did not see me until it was on me and then it screeched and its claws raked my chest.

I remember hearing shouting from below. A bright beam spun its cone around and then centered on me. This happened just as I fell with the owl. My perch had been precarious, and it did not take much to topple me, especially since I was so occupied with trying to tear the bird's claws loose from its painful clutch on my chest.

As I have said, there is something about me, my "magnetic moment," which has tended to cause coincidences which would be incredible in fiction to occur around me. It has given me very good luck many times.

But we have to pay with good for bad; for every action there is an opposite and equal reaction.

Bad fortune came. I fell a hundred feet, and this time, if my brain had not been frozen by the horror of it, I would have thought that I had come to the end of a long and unusually interesting trail. I could not expect to survive two long falls in the same day, even if this was much shorter than the first.

Rifles shot at me even as I fell. The owl screamed and tore itself loose and then it exploded in feathers. A bullet or two had hit it.

The bright lights and the dark green-black top of the tent expanded before me, whirled to one side, came back, shot away, the wind whistled through my ears, the rifles barked, and I kept my mouth closed, determined even then not to give them the pleasure of hearing me scream.

Then I was unconscious.

When I opened my eyes, I saw that it was still night. I was surprised, not because it was night but because I had expected to be dead.

By then the tent on which I had fallen had been set up again. I had hit it on my back with my legs and arms extended sidewise. The top had caved in but not lightly. I had hit the ground, but the impact had been considerably softened by the tent. Not enough so that my muscles did not ache but not enough to break any bones.

I was lying on my side inside a ring formed by six guards with rifles pointing at me. My hands were handcuffed behind me, and my legs just above the ankles had irons locked around them. The irons were connected by a thick chain of duraluminum or similar alloy. Moreover, something had been secured around my waist—it felt like another duraluminum chain—and a plastic disc about six inches in diameter and an inch thick was held against my belly by the belt. My belt with its knife had been removed, of course.

Murtagh stood near me but just outside the nearest guard. He bent over to look at me more closely. His eyes were as empty of light as a dead man's. His jaws protruded apishly, and his head moved from side to side, repulsively and, I am sure, compulsively.

"Lord Grandrith," he said. "The one and only. *Pelus blancus simiarum*. The demon of the jungle. Last of the wild men. Lord of the trees. Pristine spirit of darkest Africa. Member of the House of Lords and one of the wealthiest men in the world."

His voice was high and harsh. There was nothing about the

man to like. He even had a bad odor, though I doubt if the others could have smelled it.

"Traitor, also!" he said. "And a corpse soon! Right now, if I had my say about it! You're far too dangerous to let live for a second!"

There did not seem to be anything to say in reply, so I glared at him.

"Before long you'll wish that I had had my way," he said. "Old Mubaniga wants you taken to the base, so taken you will be. And when the Nine get their hands on you, you know what to expect."

It was cool in the night on the soft dank ground of the rain forest, but I was sweating. I was not afraid, but I do have a vivid imagination and I could visualize some of the things that would be done to me.

Murtagh said, "The mathematical probabilities for your having survived just the explosion of the plane, let alone the fall into the sea, are so small that… well, and then… Do you know, you are the only man ever to have reduced me to stuttering. Congratulations for that. Though there will be nothing else from now on to congratulate you for."

He looked hard at me, turned, and went into the tent. A man pulled the flap of the tent down. I rolled over without objection from the guards and looked around. Beyond my six guards were four more, stationed as backups. There did not seem to be anything I could do. I did not even test the handcuffs, since I was sure that even I could not break the metal of the links. And if I could, then what?

I closed my eyes and in a short time was asleep. This

ability to relax is beast-like, and, as my biographer pointed out innumerable times, I am half-beast.

A hand shook me awake. I should have heard the man approach and smelled him, but I was utterly exhausted. I had had a hard day.

The man was Murtagh. He had come out of his tent a few minutes after I was asleep. I wondered if keeping me awake was going to be the first part of the torture. But he only smiled, managing to look even more reptilian, and he said, "Aren't you curious about the disc attached to your belly?"

I did not reply. He sneered and said, "It's an explosive which contains a radio receiver. If you should by any chance get loose, you would not get far."

He took a small metal case and said, "If I snap the pseudo-lighter, the transmitter in the case will send out a frequency which will be detected by the receiver in the explosive. And your belly, and the rest of you, will be blown to little pieces. There will not be enough for the small birds to eat. And even if you should, somehow, get the handcuffs off, and then, somehow, detach the belt, you could not remove the disc without tearing off the skin of your belly. It is bonded with epoxy glue to your skin."

It seemed to me that the range of the transmitter would be limited. But I said nothing.

Murtagh hesitated and then said, grinning, "Oh, yes. I almost forgot. I was one of the ten candidates chosen to replace you and Caliban. If I capture or kill you, I was to be one of two. The other, I suppose, will be the man who gets Caliban. And that may be I, since I will be allowed to go after him once I've turned you over to the proper authority. In which case, I am bound to sit with the Nine."

I remained silent. He bared his lips, showing thick yellow teeth, and made a sucking noise as if he were going to spit on me. But he turned again, and the flap over the tent fell down. Within a few seconds, I was once more asleep.

At six in the morning, I was awakened. I had been half-awake for some time during the night because it had rained. The canopy kept much of the rain from falling directly onto me, but drops and occasional trickles startled me from a deep sleep. However, I am accustomed to this; even a more extreme change of temperature and humidity would not have made me suffer much. The guards around me complained about having to stand outside, but they did so in low voices that showed they did not wish Murtagh to hear.

A few minutes after the whistle sounded to wake the camp, Murtagh appeared from the tent. He stared at me a minute as if to satisfy himself that I was still there or to gloat over his reward for catching me. Then he went back in, and I heard the whirr of the electric razor. Breakfast was cooked in cans over the heater, and the cuffs were taken off my wrists so I could feed myself. Six men still guarded me. After eating, I rose and stretched and bent this way and that to get the kink and the pain out of my muscles. I was still sore from the fall, and being forced to sleep in the cramped chained-up position had not relieved me.

I submitted to having my hands cuffed behind me again, since there was nothing else I could do. My leg irons were taken off, and I was allowed to pace back and forth. During this time, the tents were quickly taken down and folded up into handkerchief size again, the support frames were collapsed, along with the furniture, and formed into small cylinders and stuck into the packs. The cans were pressed flat under the heavy boots of the men and then piled into a heap with other debris and garbage. A man sprinkled a fluid from a container onto the pile, smoke curled up from the pile material; the whole took on a gray cast, changed to ashes, and collapsed. The ashes were blown about, and we marched away with no sign of a large camp having been there. The footprints and the holes left by the stakes had been pressed down by men wearing broad discs on their boots.

The march was led by Murtagh, who frequently consulted his compass and also a small device which he held to his ear. These were guiding him through the rain forest, and it was fortunate that he had them. It is easy for anybody except a native to get lost in the forest. By native, I do not mean the average African native. He shuns these places; he hates to venture into the arched columnar world. The pygmies and the anthropoids and The Folk and the beasts of the quiet green mansions know their way around. And I know.

I did not understand why Murtagh did not lead us back the way he had come, since it was only about six miles to the edge of the forest. But he seemed to know what he was doing. And, after a half a day's journey, we broke out of the forest into a clearing. This was a recent, man-made well into which helicopters could drop. A few minutes later, a Sikorsky S-62 appeared and settled down. My leg irons were replaced, and I was forced to hop to the craft and climb awkwardly in. Murtagh and twelve of his officers got in, and we took off. Apparently the copter would return to pick up the others in several trips. It was some satisfaction to me that I had destroyed so many of their copters that they were reduced to one.

This was not true. After a twenty-minute trip, as registered by Murtagh's wristwatch, we came over another clearing. This was also man-made but much larger. There were about forty large tents arranged in concentric circles and, to one side, a space for copters. Two small craft squatted there. There was no sign of jets or of a landing strip for them.

Murtagh had sat ahead of me. He did not speak a single word during the flight. Once, he looked back at me and smiled. He seemed self-congratulatory, as a "great white hunter" would who was returning with the head of the largest elephant ever shot. The others did not speak either. I would have thought they would be much more jubilant, and then it occurred to me that they might be dreading reprimand or punishment of some kind. After all, they had not been so efficient; they had allowed one man to decimate them. And I had been caught, not through their cunning, but by sheer accident.

Why did Murtagh, their leader, the man responsible, not share their feelings?

Perhaps he did not care if he was reprimanded, since he had achieved his mission. And that, really, was all the Nine required of their servants.

After I had clambered out, my leg irons were removed. Murtagh removed the transmitter-activator from his pocket, showed it to me as he smiled slightly, and then gestured at my guards to conduct me ahead of him. We went through three circles of tents and stopped before the tent which was the center of the circles. This was also the largest, being thirty feet high. There were four guards in front and two at each corner outside the tent. When we went inside, I saw two at each interior corner.

A wall of cloth made two rooms. Murtagh reported to the officer at the table before the wall and presented a small plastic card. I'm sure that the officer knew Murtagh quite well, but he still went through the established procedures. He inserted the card into a small metal box with a screen above it. I could not see what the screen showed, but its presentation satisfied the officer. He picked up a wireless phone and said that he would send in Doctor Murtagh and the prisoner. He listened for a moment and then put up the phone.

"Give me the activator," the officer said, pointing at the device.

Murtagh did not say anything or move at all for a few seconds except for the sidewise oscillation of his head. He opened his mouth as if to protest but checked himself. The officer took the activator and went through the flap over the entrance in the wall. When he returned, he no longer had the device.

Evidently whoever was to receive us wanted to make sure that he controlled any detonation of the explosives in the disc glued to my belly. I admired his caution. If I had been he, I would have made certain that such an ambitious man as Murtagh did not get a chance to blow up the prisoner along with his superior and claim it was an accident or had to be done to keep me from escaping.

There was really little chance that Murtagh would do that, since he had half-won his seat at the table of the Nine. But the person within had survived so many millennia by not taking unnecessary chances.

This was Mubaniga.

He sat in a high-backed folding chair at a large folding

desk. Leopard skins cushioned his thin wrinkled flesh and frail millennia-old bones. His kinky hair was white, and his face and hands were valleys and ridges of grayish-black skin. The sunken eyes were black with red streaks mixed with yellow. His teeth were very thick and widely spaced. He wore a white jumpsuit with a black scarf around his age-corroded neck.

This was Mubaniga, one of the Nine. I had seen him at least once a year for fifty-seven years. Each time except one he had always been remote, and the meeting had been brief enough though painful for me. This was during the annual ceremony when a piece of flesh was extracted from the candidates and the elixir was given in return. But when I was the Speaker for the Nine, a sort of major-domo for several months, I came into more intimate contact with the Nine. Mubaniga had never talked to me except to give me orders now and then. But I had stood by and listened while the Nine talked among themselves. And often he talked to himself in a language which had to be the ancestor of all the Bantu and semi-Bantu languages spoken in Africa today.

I have the most intimate practical knowledge of African languages of any man, white or black, and also have a Ph.D. in African Linguistics from the University of Berlin. My doctoral thesis (unpublished so far) was in fact derived from what I learned indirectly from Mubaniga. I got so I could understand some small part of what he muttered to himself, and I established a linguistic connection between proto-Bantu and the language of a small inland New Guinea tribe I had come across during World War II. My thesis was that the Negroids had originated in southeastern Asia, possibly in some parts of southeastern India, and had spread out in two directions. One branch had migrated to Africa and evolved into the Negro types we know now; the other had migrated to New Guinea and Melanesia and evolved into the types now existing. Those who had stayed in the land of origin had been absorbed into the Caucasoid and Mongoloid population.

Mubaniga, of course, had been born long after the migrations had taken place, even if he was twenty to twenty-five thousand years old. But he remembered the legends and the myths and the folk tales about those migrations in the days when there was a land bridge between south Arabia and Africa.

The Negroes had been diverted southward by the whites who lived in North Africa and had killed or absorbed the ancestors of the Hottentots and Bushmen.

My thesis was almost rejected. I knew it was based on valid evidence, but I could not produce Mubaniga as my witness. But the German doctors finally agreed that I did have some slight linguistic evidence, enough to call it brilliant but not really conclusive.

So now ancient Mubaniga sat before me and looked at me with eyes as fiery cold as a leopard's. He could speak a wretched English but addressed me in Swahili, which he spoke a little better. My own Swahili is perfect.

"At last," he said, "you have come to the end of the long road. Long for you, I suppose, but it seems a short one to me."

He could say that without contradiction.

I shrugged and said, "Once you're dead, what's the difference whether you have lived thirty thousand years or were born dead? To you, there is no difference. And if I have come to the end of my road, yours is not too far off."

Mubaniga cackled. He held up the activator and said, "Since the end is so close for me, I might as well press this. It will remove you and me and everybody in this tent and quite a few people outside."

Murtagh must have understood Swahili, because he drew in air with a hiss and paled.

The ancient put down the activator, though he kept his hand on it. He said, "You would have made a fine man to sit at the table. You are as cunning as the hare and as strong as the leopard, and you have a hyena's ability to survive. You might have sat at the table for thirty thousand years, as Anana has. But no, you had to throw away all that just because you could not stomach some deeds which have no significance for immortals. Don't you know that these people you pity will all be dead within a few years? Nothing you can do to them can really hurt them or deserves your pity. The only important thing is that you will live almost forever. What happens to the others does not matter."

"I understand the philosophy," I said. "But Caliban and I have self-respect, and we were choking on what you were shoving down our throats."

He shrugged and said, "Other candidates have felt the same way, and they died because they tried to fight us."

He spoke in Swahili to Murtagh. "You won't have to use the drugs to find out where Caliban is. Our agents have seen him in Gramzdorf, West Germany. But it is evident that both of them have an organization they're using against us. You will extract all the information from Grandrith about this. And then you will go to Germany to take charge of the hunt there, unless Caliban is caught before you are through with Grandrith, of course."

"Thank you very much, sir," Murtagh said. The only visible effect the news had was to slightly increase the sidewise oscillations of his head.

Mubaniga smiled and said, "You may thank me within the next hour, if you can."

Murtagh's oscillations stopped for a minute. I thought that his skin became even paler. I did not know what Mubaniga meant, but I soon found out. Contrary to what I'd expected, I was not at once conducted to a tent where the drugs would be injected. Instead, I was fed at noon, and then was conducted to one side of the clearing. A chair was brought outside for Mubaniga. He still held the activator. About forty feet before us were twenty-five eight-foot high posts. I was led toward the posts but was stopped by my guards ten feet from them.

Then Murtagh and twenty-four men, all stripped to the waist, were led out under guard. Smith, the radio operator whose life I'd spared, was among them. They faced the posts while their hands were tied above them to the tops. A man whose name I later found out was Greenrigg approached them with a long whip. He was six feet six and weighed probably three hundred. He had a paunch of no great size and a sheathing of fat, but if he had dieted he still would have weighed two hundred and seventy.

He raised the whip at a signal from Mubaniga. The first lash was on Murtagh's back and brought blood from a deep gash. Greenrigg then went on to the next man and down the line. He returned to Murtagh for the second round. Ten lashes were delivered to all except Smith. By then, some men were screaming and some were groaning and some had fainted. Murtagh stood upright and silent, and when he was untied he walked slowly and dignifiedly to the medical tent to have his wounds treated and bandaged. The others, however, were not permitted to leave immediately. They had to watch Greenrigg whip Smith until he died. No one told me why he was treated so, but I knew enough of the Nine to guess why. He had allowed himself to be taken prisoner by an enemy of the Nine, and they did not know what, if anything, he had told me. They could have found out by using the drugs they planned for me. But this would have taken time. Besides it was a good object lesson to the others to kill him so painfully.

Murtagh had not been relieved of his position, since he had attained the Nine's goal. But he had not conducted the operation to the complete satisfaction of the Nine and so must pay. Undoubtedly, if he did not do any better with Caliban, he might lose his candidate's position or even his life.

One of the men who had not been whipped because he had not been a member of the original force made a mistake. He taunted Murtagh with his inefficiency. Murtagh pulled out his automatic and put a .45 into his heart. Mubaniga said nothing about this. Murtagh was within his rights. He had paid for his mistakes and, since he had not been demoted, he was to be treated with the respect due an officer of the Nine.

I was immediately chained down by the legs to an eyebolt in the floor of one of the small helicopters. Murtagh and two others accompanied me. We lifted up while Mubaniga stood by the door of the big copter and watched us. The last I saw of him was a small black-faced white-suited figure. I wondered if I would ever see him again, and hoped that if I did I would be holding his neck between my hands. Even in that situation, I was still an optimist. I was not yet dead.

We flew about five hundred feet above the solid green roof for two hundred miles and then landed by the side of a strip cut out of the forest. We were transferred to a two-jet British plane which held six passengers. I was again chained by my leg irons to an eyebolt in the floor, but my hands were cuffed before me. Murtagh, I noticed, had the activator back. It must have been handed to him just before he stepped into the copter. He was not likely to use it on the plane, but I was even less likely to have a chance to force him to use it.

We ate. Night came. I slept. A man called my name, and I awoke just before the jet began to let down for a landing. This strip had also been cut out of rain forest. It originally had been fairly level land at the bottom of a valley. From the high mountains around us, the valley might still be far above sea level. The jet had to come in between two mountains forming a narrow pass and the strip itself was almost to the sides of the precipitous walls. There was barely room for the jet to taxi around so it could take off.

The strip was brilliantly lit, however, and a number of men, mostly blacks, received us. We got into a jeep and drove on a narrow road by the side of the strip out of the valley and to the right around the mountain. This took us up along the mountain. The driver, a Zanzibarian wearing a fez, sped like a maniac along the dangerous road with the right wheels often a few inches from a sheer dropoff. Finally Murtagh, whose back had been making him wince, told the driver to slow down. Murtagh was not suffering as much as he would if he had not been a servant of the Nine. The ointment was swiftly healing the lash wounds and deadened most of the pain. It was another product of Caliban's genius and would have been a boon to the world if it could have gotten it. But this, like so many of Caliban's inventions, was restricted for use among those who served the Nine. I suppose that the ancients of the oaken table liked to keep such things for themselves. Also, if Caliban had been allowed to reveal a small fraction of his inventions, he would have been the most famous man in the world. The Nine did not want him publicized. In fact, Caliban's original career as a brain surgeon at a prominent New York hospital had been cut short by the Nine. He had attracted too much attention with his great skill and the new techniques and tools he introduced.

The jeep went along so slowly then that we could talk easily. Murtagh said, "You answered every question and we have already radioed the information. Your men will be scooped up. Caliban will soon be caught."

"You mean that you drugged me on the plane?"

The reflection of the headlights from the grayish mountain walls on our left lit up his features. He smiled and said, "Yes. The drug was in your food. Even so, you were a reluctant subject. I had to use all my knowledge to dredge up the information. But you talked. And the men you've been using will be taken."

"They had no idea they were fighting the Nine," I said. "In fact, as far as I know, they have never heard of the Nine."

He shrugged. "It doesn't matter. They were helping you against us."

The men had known they could be in great danger if they helped me. They had been well paid, and they were expecting to die if things did not go well. But I still felt that, in some obscure sense, I had betrayed them. Rationally, I knew that I could not have helped talking. Knowing that did not erase a sense of guilt.

His statement that Caliban would soon be caught could not be based on anything I had told him. Caliban has his own organization, and while there was verbal contact between his men and mine, there was no way for Murtagh to find a path leading from my men to Caliban's.

Then I suppressed a groan. Murtagh must have seen some tremor and guessed the thought that made me sick.

"Oh, yes, you told us where your wife was."

He waited. Seeing that I would not reply, he added, "If it's any consolation to you, we'll be bringing her to you. We wouldn't want to separate a man and his wife."

There was always the chance that Clio might get away, but I told only myself that. He was not going to get any satisfaction out of my responses if I could help it.

But I was so furious—though more at myself than at him—that I might have seized him and jumped over the side of the trail and down the mountain, if I had been able. But my hands had been cuffed behind me and my legs were chained to an eyebolt on the jeep floor. And Murtagh and another man held pistols on me.

Murtagh said, "There is no doubt about the great capabilities of yourself and Caliban. Of course, you should have been candidates. But the fact that XauXaz was your grandfather must have been the main reason why you two were picked to fight for his seat."

He could not have known that unless he had questioned me while I was drugged. He was playing a dangerous game, since the Nine did not like inquiries into their personal business. But then any man who qualified as candidate for a seat at the table did not lack guts.

That he felt it necessary to reassure himself that nepotism was the chief basis for the choice of Caliban and me revealed much about his own self-doubts, however. That he could not resist telling me that he knew that XauXaz was our grandfather added more light to his character.

The sky began to pale above the jagged peaks on our right. The road led downward, and by the time we'd reached the bottom of the mountain, dawn had filled the valley. The road went through a semi-desert area. There was so little evidence of rainfall that I wondered if we were near the back parts of the mountains which hid the caverns of the Nine. There is rain forest on all sides of this range, but a freakish climatic condition carries rains over or around the mountains here.

Presently we were stopped by a gate in a wall which blocked the narrow valley. Above the mortared stone ramparts were sentinel towers, and three machine guns and a Bofors rapid-fire cannon stuck out from embrasures. The man on the driver's left got out and stuck a card through a slit in the wall. After a minute, the gates swung open. The jeep drove through; the metal gates, which were twelve feet high, swung shut. The road wound through a camp of the exceedingly light tents. I counted thirty men there and twenty at the wall. Then we were past the tents and going down. The mountains on both sides pressed in.

I had wondered why a copter had not lifted us over or around the mountain. But if this was indeed the rear entrance to the caves, then copters or any aircraft might be forbidden. That did not seem likely. Murtagh, at that moment, answered a call on the radio and at the same time answered my question. Some observers ahead, who were hidden from us, were asking for identification again. The security measures here were very strict indeed, and this was one more piece of evidence that the caves were nearby. Murtagh identified himself and the party and then said something about when copters would arrive. It was evident from the conversation that followed that they were in short supply. I did not know why, but I surmised that important missions (among which may have been my capture) had taken them from this area.

We passed under a projection of gray, red-speckled granite. Holes had been cut in the face and in the bottom of the rock, and from these the white and black faces of guards looked. When I was past the projection, I looked back and upward. About a hundred feet above the outthrust was a dark opening containing armed men. That could be the rear entrance to the caves. The surface of the mountainside was so smooth that I suspected it was man-made. And from the opening to as high as I could see, the mountain leaned outward.

A helicopter could not have gotten close enough to the entrance to deliver passengers. Some sort of crane would have to drop a lift to hoist people up. If there was an elevator shaft within the mountain, its entrance at the base of the mountain was well-hidden.

The jeep drove on around the shoulder of the mountain. After two miles on a rough dirt road, the jeep stopped. Here the mountains were even closer. The sun would not be seen most of the day, and at this time a pale twilight filled the bottom of the valley with a seemingly liquid light.

The jeep stopped. The men got out. The chains through the eyebolt were unlocked, and I was told to get out. We marched down the road, which was too narrow now for even a jeep to traverse. After two minutes, we were challenged again. The post here consisted of four men. A few feet beyond them, the path stopped. Beyond was a sheer dropoff of two hundred feet.

A thousand feet to the north, the two mountains merged.

Murtagh shoved his gun into my back and forced me to the edge. I looked down. The floor of the canyon was mostly bare rock with a few plants growing alongside a stream about six feet wide. The source of the stream was a small lake at the extreme end, and this derived from a spring, I supposed. The water ran down the middle of the canyon floor and then disappeared in the base of the cliff on which I stood. The only signs of habitation were three small huts built of stone halfway along the eastern wall.

A motor roared to my right. I turned to see a truck backing out of a cave. Its bed held a crane and a large drum of cable. At the end of the cable was a sling of leather. Evidently, I was supposed to sit in it so I could be lowered to the bottom of the canyon.

Murtagh, his face moving slightly from side to side, his thin lips pulled back to show long yellow teeth, watched while my cuffs were removed. I flexed my arms and did some knee bends. Then, at a gesture from him, I got into the sling. I could do nothing with all those guns aimed at me. The truck backed up until its wheels were close to the edge of the precipice, and I hung in the air past the edge. The motor and the cable drum worked, and I was lowered swiftly to the bottom. While I went down, I noted that the sides of the canyon inclined outward and were very smooth. If there had been any roughnesses which could be used for handholds, or any projections, they had been removed.

I got out of the sling, and it rose up quickly. Faces sticking out over the edge were small white or black pie plates. This hole was to be my prison until the day of judgment. Evidently they were not worried that I would try to kill myself. They knew me well enough.

I smelled the water and tasted it. It seemed to be excellent drinking water. I started walking along the stream. When I came to a point opposite the stone huts, I stopped. I smelled a human female and that of another creature which I could not identify for a moment. Then the hackles on my neck rose, or felt as if they did, and I growled automatically. A male of The Folk was inside the hut.

A woman stuck her head out of the hut and seeing me, called "John!" She stepped out then, but I knew who she was as soon as I heard her voice. She was the six-foot one-inch high titian-haired beauty, the Danish Countess Clara Aekjaer. The last time I had seen her was at the annual ceremony eight months ago. She was dressed exactly as she had been then. She had no makeup, but she really did not need any.

She walked toward me with all the "vibrations made free" that Eve must have had for Adam. She was smiling as if she thought I had come to deliver her from this place.

I could not pay much attention to her just then because I was concentrating on the occupant of the other hut. He had stuck his head out, confirming what my sense of smell had informed me.

I did not know him, which was not surprising, since The Folk of the mountains in eastern Africa have always been very few and very shy. In fact, I had thought they were now extinct, with the possible exception of one female. Eight months ago, I had been forced to kill a male, *shth-tb* or Leopard-Breaker, as the name translates somewhat freely. He was the last male of his species, I had thought, and since his child was dying, his female would die without issue. But here was a big and apparently healthy male.

He came out into the twilight which filled the box canyon and stood before the entrance of the stone hut for a moment. He was about six feet three and probably carried three hundred and eighty pounds on that massive skeleton. Long russet hairs covered a dark brown skin. Actually, he had fewer hairs than a human, just as a chimpanzee has fewer, but their length made him seem hairier. His body was humanoid except for the relatively shorter legs and longer arms. His feet were not those of ape's but more like the feet of Neanderthal Man. He had the rounded buttocks and pelvic structure which would cause an anthropologist to unhesitatingly classify him as hominid. He never walked on fours, like a gorilla, as my biographer described the walking posture of The Folk. But my biographer did not know all the facts when he wrote the first two volumes of my life and so drew more on his imagination than on anything. Later, though he discovered his error, he clung to it to maintain consistency.

The neck was thick and powerful. The face was, at first glance, gorilloid, and I suppose a layman would continue to think of it as so after a long familiarity with it. Though I can't imagine any human except myself wanting to maintain close contact with it unless there were bars between him and the male. The immense ridges of bone above the eyes, the flat, wide-nostriled nose, the protruding jaws, the undeveloped chin, the thin black lips, and the long yellow canines, plus the low forehead and the roach of hair on top of his head would have frightened, or at least made uneasy, most humans. He looked much like the reconstructions of Paranthropus, the big vegetarian hominid that lived a million years ago in East Africa. He was basically vegetarian, too, but his teeth were more like those of the gorilla, who is not a meat eater. But The Folk eat meat whenever they can get it. He's an anomaly because his teeth are more apish than human, yet his brain is larger than a gorilla's. And he has a language. He is the living basis of African folk tales, a giant variety of the little hairy men the East African natives call *agogwe*.

He rolled toward me, swaying from side to side, his arms hanging loose but the huge black-brown hands working. His paunch stuck out before him, and the massive chest rose and fell swiftly.

I spoke to him in the whispering speech of The Folk. He stopped and blinked, then continued. I spoke again. He stopped again, and he said, "What language is that?"

I was astonished. No wonder. He spoke English. The pronunciation was not accurate, but the structure of his mouth would prevent the exact reproduction of a number of English phones. And he often did not voice his vowels of *u* in *untamed* or *o* in *son* or the second *a* in *galaxy*. But he spoke as fluently as if English were his native tongue, which it was. He had never heard the speech of The Folk before.

His bearing was not aggressive. I had just assumed it was, since all male of The Folk, on meeting strangers, act belligerently whether they feel so or not. He was merely approaching me to talk to me and was prepared to speak English or Swahili.

What he could not explain, Clara could. Twenty years ago, an agent of the Nine had brought him in when he was a few days old. The mother had died of some disease. Under direct orders of the Nine, Dick, as he was called, had been raised with the children of two Kenyans who were agents for the Nine. He had lived a good part of his twenty years on the edge of the rain forest of the mountains along the east Congo border. When he was twelve, he had been sent to this area.

For what purpose?

"Ah, John," Clara said, putting her long-fingered hand on my arm, "I suspect the Nine thought they would have some use for him eventually. And the eventual has come. I think they mean to put you two together in an arena of some sort, where you will be torn to pieces, if things work out as they expect."

"Is that true?" I said to Dick.

"I don't know," he said. "A man kept calling me names and throwing stones at me when he thought I wasn't looking. And he put stuff in my food to make me sick. I didn't see him do it, but I knew he did it. He hated me for some reason, though I had never done anything to him. I complained to my superior, and he told the man to lay off me. But this man, Scannon, he kept on bugging me. So, one day, when I crawled into bed and found a poisonous snake there, with no way for it to get there unless someone put it in my bed, I got very angry. I hit Scannon. I didn't mean to kill him, but I broke his jaw and his neck. And they put me down here, even though I told them it wasn't my fault."

It was strange to hear one of The Folk speaking English. Actually, though he was born of them, he could not be considered one of The Folk in any except a genetic sense.

Clara said, "I don't think he was put down here because he killed Scannon. That was just an excuse."

"And what do you think?"

"I think he's our jailer. Yours, rather, since they wouldn't really expect me to be able to escape from this place. And I think that it would be just like the Nine to pit Dick against you for their own amusement."

She could be right. On the other hand, he could be telling the truth, and *she* could have been set here to keep an eye on me. Or not so much to watch me as to pump me for information that Murtagh and the drug hadn't been able to get. The drug works well, but the one being questioned gives very restricted answers. And if the questioner doesn't ask the proper question, and word them just right, he isn't going to get much. Perhaps the Nine, knowing my fondness for Clara, hoped she would get me to talking.

I didn't ask her why she was imprisoned, expecting that she would volunteer soon enough. And so she did, though with a tone of exasperation at my seeming lack of curiosity.

She had been sent on a mission for the Nine to Rio de Janeiro. But she had delayed leaving London immediately because she was in love with an Englishman. So she had been drugged and put into a plane and shipped here. She supposed she would be an object lesson for the servants of the Nine in some hideous fashion. She did not seem to be frightened at the prospect, but Clara was a very courageous woman. Or perhaps she just did not care. She was a wild woman, one who lived intensely for every moment and was reckless of consequences.

But she was intelligent and she must know what could be in store for her. Also, she could be a plant, as I said.

"You knew what would happen if you did not follow orders at once," I said. "You really have no one but yourself to blame."

"But I was passionately in love!" she cried.

I smiled. Clara was always in love, although she seldom stayed in that state long with one man.

At noon, the food was lowered to us in a net tied to the cable. We were given no utensils to use, on the theory that they might be adapted to make tools or weapons, I suppose. The food was good, though cooked too much for my taste. Dick was given meat along with the bamboo shoots, nuts, berries, and bananas. During the meal, I asked him if he wished to join me in an attempt to escape. It did not hurt to ask him, I thought, since even if he had been placed there to watch me, I would be expected to try escaping. And if he relayed the information to my captors, he would have to be quick and sly about it to get by me.

The same reasoning applied to Clara.

"Yes," Dick said, peering out from under the massive frontal bones. "I want to escape. These are bad men. But where do we go? Even if we can get away, which we can't."

That was difficult to answer. He certainly couldn't settle down with any group of natives I knew. They would kill him or sell him to scientists. He could not go into the wilds, because he did not know how to survive there. He would have been as lost and helpless as a European astray in the rain forest.

"Well," I said, "if those canines were removed, and you were shaved all over and put into a suit of clothes, you might be able to pass for an unusually ugly specimen of humanity—no offence intended. You could make a fortune as a wrestler or boxer. I could introduce you to an honest manager, relatively honest, anyway. But you wouldn't be happy there, and sooner or later some zoologist would look closely at you, and the game would be up. Besides, city life would sicken you, you couldn't stand the gas fumes, the factory stinks, the noise, the crowds, but..."

I shouldn't have told him all that. I needed him, and it wouldn't help any to discourage him with the truth. If he had been a human being, I would have lied to him. But he was one of The Folk, and even though I have loved only two members of that genus, tolerated some others, and hated most, I could not lie to this simple trusting soul. That is, if he was as open and simple as he seemed to be. I had to remind myself that he could be a cunning agent for the Nine.

"There was a time when you could have lived with me on my plantation in Kenya," I said. "But I lost that, and I can't ever return to Kenya, not unless I'm disguised. But I'll think of something. The important thing is to get out of here. As soon as possible."

"If anyone could do it, you could," Clara said. "Or maybe Caliban. But nobody can. You'd have to be a bird to get out of here."

At dusk our supper was lowered. We went into a stone hut to eat and talk. There was no furniture there except for a pail to throw our garbage into. Our only bedding was a pile of old blankets, but these sufficed to keep us warm, with the help of each other's body heat. Back of the hut was a latrine ditch. As soon as night fell, and it fell early here, while the sky, three thousand feet above, was still a dark blue, we left the hut. The south end was lit by powerful beams, and a searchlight probed the valley. But we walked to the far north end, ignoring the light when it followed us. I plunged into the pool, sixty feet long and thirty wide, at the base of the northern wall. The water was icy, but I waded waist-deep until I got near to the wall, where I had to dive down. There were several openings in the rock through which water bubbled. But all were too small for me to get into.

After thoroughly exploring the bottom, I got out. I ran all the way to the other end to dry myself and warm up. Dick and Clara followed me at a brisk walk.

I was visible to the men above in the lights glaring down. They could see what I was doing, and if they wished to stop me, they had the means. But I think they were just laughing at me. I went into the tiny pool there and dived down to the bottom. This was about thirty feet deep, and the water flowed through an opening about six feet across. But a thick metal screen had been affixed to the rock with many metal spikes. I tugged at the screen about a dozen times, coming up for air each time. By the time I gave up, I was half-frozen, and it took me a long time to stop shivering. Somebody at the top of the cliff hooted at me for my efforts.

However, I did not feel that I had been foolish or wasted my time. That they had felt it necessary to screen the hole indicated that the hole might be an escape route.

After I had gotten warm under the blankets between Clara and Dick, I crawled out. Dick wanted to sleep; despite being raised by humans, he was one of The Folk in being unable to look far into the future. I told him he might lose more sleep before we got out of this, and if we didn't he'd have as long to sleep as anybody ever wished for. Grumbling, he followed me out. We sneaked past the probing searchlight to the detritus of flint I had seen at the northeast corner. Apparently, it had fallen there when a projection was blown off about fifty feet up.

Since there was no light, I could not work the flint. But when dawn came, I went to the door of the hut with a blanket over my shoulders. By the dim light there, I hammered and chipped away until I had several handaxes, long stabbing knives, scrapers, and choppers. I had learned the techniques from a French anthropologist who was once a guest at Grandrith Manor.

"What do you plan to do with your Early Paleolithic weapons, my cave man?" Clara said.

"I don't know yet," I said. That was true, but if I had a plan, I would not have told her until just before I initiated it.

"Well, at least you're keeping out of mischief."

The day passed just like it had before, except that Dick and I dived down to the bottom of the outlet pool and strove to pull the screen loose. When we came up for air, we could look up and see the faces of our guards there. They did not fire down to drive us away. It may be they felt there was no slightest chance of our loosening the screen. And if we wanted to exercise and to provide them with some slight amusement in a deadly dull job, so be it.

We gave up after a dozen dives. If our combined strength could not pull a corner of the screen loose with our bare hands, then tools were needed. I spent the rest of the day traveling around the base of the canyon and examining the walls. The northeast corner formed an almost square junction. By putting my back against one wall and pushing with my feet against the other, at a difficult angle, I might be able to inch my way up for the first hundred feet. After that the walls leaned slightly outward until, near the top, they were at an angle of about eighty-two degrees from the horizontal. The corner still maintained its squareness, but I would have to exert a tremendous pressure to keep from falling. I was not sure at all that I could do it.

As far as I could tell, there were no guards on that side.

Two hours before dusk, two men holding rapid-fire rifles were lowered. They stood guard while their officer, a Lal Singh, rode down. Then two other riflemen rode down. Then a man with scuba gear.

We three prisoners were allowed to stand within forty feet and watch them. The scubaman came up with a satisfactory report. Then our huts were examined. They did not find the flint weapons because I had hidden them beneath the surface of the north pool. The scubaman did not look into that pool. Evidently they knew that I could do nothing there.

After making searches at random in other parts of the canyon, they left. Just before he was hauled away, I asked Singh what had happened to Murtagh. He did not reply. I surmised that Murtagh had been sent to Germany after Caliban. Probably nothing would be done with me until he was killed or captured. But I could not bank on that. If Clio was caught and brought here, the Nine might think there were enough victims for a Roman holiday.

As soon as it was dark, I sneaked out and cut down some of the hardwood bushes. I trimmed them off and sharpened their points. I still did not know what to do with them, but if a situation arose where they would be handy, they would be waiting and ready. And they could be used as pitons, if I found a big enough crack.

I wanted to tell Clara and Dick what I planned. If their stories were true, then they should be with me. I did not think that Clara, strong though she was, could manage that climb. Dick was powerful enough, stronger than me, but he was also much heavier. And I just could not chance that they were spies. That the men had come down to search the area did not mean that either of my fellow prisoners had informed on me, of course. Almost everything I had done had been visible. And if my flint tools had been discovered, I might have suspected that I had been betrayed. No, they would say nothing about the flint.

An hour after nightfall, I slipped out from the blankets. Clara and Dick both stirred, and Dick said something, in Swahili, in his sleep. I stood there for a while, made sure they were deeply asleep, or else pretending to be, and left with my sticks. I waited a while by a bush to see if anybody would follow me. No one did. The beams probed around at random. I avoided them, went to the north pool, and recovered my flint weapons.

Before starting the climb, I had to get rid of the plastic bomb stuck to my belly with epoxy glue. I began chipping away at it with a flint dagger. The disc had a two-inch diameter and was two-tenths of an inch thick. The plastic was very hard and not easy to get at because of its snug position between my belly and the metal belt, which was two inches broad. I had to bring the flint down with considerable force to chip away the plastic. For all I knew, the concussion could set it off, though it did not seem likely that an unstable explosive would be used.

As I found out, the plastic was a rather thin shell around

a tiny radio receiver and the tiny chemical detonating cylinder attached to the receiver. The problem became ticklish when I got to the detonator—not literally, of course. It was probable that a hard blow could set that off. So I pried away around it. The darkness and the angle at which I had to look at it made the task more difficult.

But, eventually, I pried both receiver and detonator loose and dropped them into the pool.

A shell of plastic was still adhering to my belly. It would have to stay there until I was able to find a chemical to cancel the bondage of the glue. And the belt was too tight for me to wriggle out of.

I had torn a strip of blanket off earlier that day. I tied this around my waist and shoved two daggers and six short sticks into a fold of the cloth. Since I would be bent forward with my back against the one wall and my legs drawn up with my feet against the other, I would keep the stone and wood from falling out.

The stone only got warmed up in winter time when the sun was directly overhead, and it lost its heat quickly. The skin of my back felt cold, at first. Later, as friction between skin and rock increased, the skin got too warm. And, of course, my back started to bleed. I left a trail of blood on the cliff wall as if I were some slug dying of hemorrhage.

To ease the rubbing away and cutting of the skin, I went slowly. But I got to the final fifty feet within an estimated twenty minutes. By then the strain was beginning to affect me. The pressure I had to maintain was draining my strength, and I was losing more blood than I had expected. Or at least it felt as if I were. The juncture of the two walls did not afford a perfect corner of a square. The walls were at oblique angles which varied, and this meant that often one leg had to be stretched out much further than the other. The unequal pressure sometimes brought me close to an uncontrollable shaking of my left leg.

Meantime, the beams continued to probe through the canyon, and several times they passed directly over me. When the cone got close, I stopped moving. The light, weak at this distance, did not reveal me to the men on the cliff, if they were watching. They must have been convinced that no one could escape. For all I knew, the searchlight was operated by a machine, and they only occasionally looked down from their card games or whatever occupied them.

I began the ascent on the part that projected outward. From that time on, I was like a fly on a ceiling. I had to be even more of a living wedge, one which proceeded by minute movements. The sliding of feet and the inching along of my back succeeded each other very slowly and very painfully. Now I bled more profusely, and my back became more slippery. The closer I got to the top, the more the cliff leaned outward. The only compensation for this was that the juncture of the two walls became more of an acute angle and thus gave me a better hold. I had planned on that, of course. If the corner had not become more narrow, I don't think I would have tried the climb. But the lesser space squeezed me down as if I were an embryo trying to give birth to myself.

I scraped across several narrow cracks in the rock but did not try to drive in any sticks as pitons. I did not need them, but when I got to the lip of the cliff, I might.

It seemed hours, but it must have been only fifteen minutes

that it took me to get up the last fifty feet. Then I was hanging over the ground, wedged in tightly, with the edge of the cliff just above me. And here, where I was closest to safety, I was in the most danger. To reach up and over to clamp a hand down on the edge meant that I had to lose my grip on the corner. I could not leap out, because that would take me away from the edge. The only thing I could do was to reach up, place my hand on the lip, which was solid rock, let loose and hang by one hand, then reach up with the other, and pull myself up and over.

First, I had to get my daggers and sticks onto the edge, if I could. Otherwise, when I straightened out, they would fall out of the fold. This required a slow withdrawal of them, one by one, from the fold, and a quick throw with a looping motion. The two flint knives clinked on the edge. Two sticks also got onto the top, but four bounced off and fell. They seemed to be striking something.

Then, without hesitation, I reached up, bent my hand so it was at right angles to my arm, spread the fingers out on the rough granite stone, and let my body sag. I could not kick myself away because my grip was too precarious. Everything had to be done quickly, yet not violently. I swung out, and my weight started to pull my hand loose, since it had nothing to hold onto but was depending on pressure alone. And even though the rock was rough, it was not knobby. The surface friction was not much.

Despite my agonized efforts with my one hand, the hand slid away, tearing off skin against the rock. I reached up with the other hand, and got its palm flat against the rock, too. For the moment I hung there, and then I lifted myself up with a slow straining that made the muscles of my back, too long tense, crack as if they were splitting wood. When my chin was above the ledge, I used it to hold me up too. In fact, my chin supported the full weight of my body for about twenty seconds while I slid my arms forward until they were fully extended and flat against the surface.

Then, scraping the skin of my chest, I inched upward and over, my fingers digging into the rock, pulling me along like the legs of Lilliputian horses. Once my chest was fully over, I kicked with my legs, and gave a final convulsive effort that pulled me up and over the edge. To crawl all the rest of the way was easy, but it seemed to take a long time.

For some time, I lay there gasping for air. The cold air made me shiver, because I was covered with sweat and with blood on my back, my hands, my chin, and my chest.

When my breathing became regular, I sat up. Just ahead of me was a six-foot high rise of rock, a tiny cliff. It was against this that the four spinning sticks had struck and bounced back and fallen over the edge. The two knives had fallen close to the edge, and I had been forced to slide over them when I pulled myself over. They had ground into my chest, but they had not cut me.

I got up, stuck the one knife and the sticks into the cloth belt, held one knife in my hand, and started to work my way along the thin ridge of the canyon top. Close at hand were the higher walls of the mountains, and I could have tried to climb them to get away. If my suspicions that this area was the back end to the caves were correct, I could go over the mountains eastward and eventually get to the front entrance. Or I could take off to the west and be out of the dry desert area and into rain-forest covered mountains where the Nine would have no chance of tracking me down.

But my original intention had been to locate and spy on the back entrance to the caves. Having familiarized myself with it, I was to meet Caliban in Europe, or wherever we could, and then we would plan our campaign. Our idea was to attack the caves during the annual ceremonies, when we knew that all of the Nine would be there. Just how our small force was to make an effective attack was something we had not yet worked out.

I had given myself about a month and a half to traverse the central part of Africa on foot, from the coast of Gabon to these mountains. Due to my enemies' participation, I had arrived six weeks sooner than planned.

The moon sailed directly over the gap between the two mountains. I slid along like a ghost from shadow to shadow, hugging the base of the mountain with the top of the box canyon a few inches to my right. I also kept watching for mines or booby-traps, but if there were any along here, I was lucky and missed them.

It took me about an hour to get to the south end of the canyon. There were times when the ledge narrowed to nothing and I had to feel along with my face pressed against the rock, my toes groping for projections, my fingers hanging onto knobs and in fissures. Then the ledge came back to existence again, and I moved swiftly.

The battery of lights along the south end was directed downward, but there was enough reflection to reveal me when I got close to the end. I went swiftly, hoping that none of the guards would see me during my brief passage.

There were four. One was sitting on a chair by the big probing searchlight, which was, as I had suspected, randomly directed by a machine. He was bundled up and drinking coffee from a thermos. Two men were in the cab of the truck. Its motor was running, so that the heater could be operated, I presumed. The fourth man was inside a tent with all flaps closed. His head and shoulders were behind a small plastic window in the side. He seemed to be at a desk, reading something.

I took the man in the chair on the edge of the cliff first. It was easy, since the truck was facing away from him, and the two men in the cab were looking away. If one had looked into a rear view mirror, he might have seen me, but that was a chance I had to take.

I did not use my flint knife. I came from behind, gripped the man's head, and twisted. The crack of the snapping spine was sharp, but no one seemed to have heard it. I relieved the man of his knife and his belt, which held ammunition and a holster with a .38 automatic. There was also a Bren machine gun by the chair.

The knife had good balance. I pulled aside the flap of the tent; the man looked around to see who it was; then he jumped up, whirling. I threw the knife, and it went deep into his throat, shutting off his cry.

The tent held a desk and a shelf full of paperbacks, a coffee-making machine, and a short-wave radio. There were also automatic rifles and boxes of ammunition, magazines, a medicine chest, tins of food, biscuits, and a small gas stove of the Caliban type.

I munched on several biscuits and drank a cup of hot coffee, which I love. Then I went out to the truck.

I was the last thing the two men expected. They must have been tough to have been selected to work for the Nine. But one man stuttered, he was so flabbergasted. The other's voice shook. Both rallied quickly enough. By the time they had gotten out of the cab, one following the other out of the left side, their hands clasped on the backs of their necks, they were tense and wary-eyed. I made them lean forward with their hands against the side of the truck, their legs and arms stiff, and then I used my knife on one. The one who had stuttered I spared.

Under my directions, he backed the truck up and then showed me how to operate the cable, and then I cuffed his hands before him. I made him sit in the cradle at the end of the cable, and then told him what he must do if he wanted to live. I had to get into the truck then, and he could have tried to swing back onto the ground and run for a rifle. But he preferred not to try for a hero's grave, and he sat still while he was lowered into the canyon. I had to get out of the truck twice to check on how far down he was. Then he trotted away toward the stone huts. After a while, the huge dark figure of Dick and the blanket-wrapped figure of Clara appeared. Getting them back up took some time but eventually it was done. The man stayed in the stone hut; I assume to make sure that I did not try to shoot him.

Clara got into the clothes of a man I'd killed. They fitted fairly well, although the boots were too large. Dick put on a coat which restricted his movements but did warm him up. They drank coffee and spooned out hot thick soup while we talked in the tent. I watched them closely, because I still did not trust them. It would have been more realistic, from my viewpoint, to leave them in the canyon, since they could be very dangerous. But, like most human beings, I am not always realistic. I value friendship and love, and I have more concern for individual human beings than my biographer indicated. However, he was basing his evaluations on my early attitudes, when I had not yet adjusted to human society and still thought of myself as one of The Folk. I can be, from a civilized point of view, horrible, but that is only when I am dealing with my enemies.

Clara put one of Caliban's quick-healing and very soothing ointments on my torn and abraded skin, and then I fitted myself out in clothes as well as I could. Clara and Dick found my story of how I had escaped almost unbelievable, but that I had rescued them and therefore had gotten out of the canyon was undeniable.

We loaded the jeep with food and ammunition. Our plan for getting away was sketchy. We would just have to drive up to the main camp and improvise from then on. If I had been alone I would have tried to find out how to get into the caves themselves, but my immediate duty was to get Dick and Clara into the rain forest. From then on, as far as I was concerned, they would be on their own, and I could return to this area.

I kept the pistol and the Bren handy at all times, and my knife was loose in its sheath. My main concern was treachery on Dick's part. Clara could be dangerous enough, but Dick, combining the enormous strength and quickness of a gorilloid hominid with all the human skills of karate and boxing and knowledge of firearms, could be the most deadly antagonist I had ever faced. So far, he had acted as if he were just what he said he was. But I wasn't going to turn my back on him.

Dick was quite capable of driving a jeep. In fact, I doubt that he could not handle anything mechanical that a human could handle. My conversations with him had been necessarily limited to practical matters, so I did not know how capable he was of really abstract thought. His brain was small, but the size of the brain is not an index of intelligence. Nor did it matter that he might not be able to appreciate the subtleties of Plato or Spinoza, Shakespeare or Joyce. How many humans can?

Clara sat in the front seat beside Dick. I was in the back seat. She drove at about twenty mph with the headlights on. We passed the cliff with the carved entrance a hundred feet up. The men stationed at the foot of the cliff did not come out to challenge us, nor was there any reason except excessive caution to make them do so. The road we were on was about sixty yards from the cliff base.

After a quarter of a mile, passing between cliffs so close we could almost reach out and touch them, we came into the open area of the main camp. There were lights at regular intervals around its perimeters; these came from lamps hung from poles. The tents all had closed flaps except one at the south end of the camp. There were four guards there, two on each side of the road, and an officer sitting at a desk within the tent.

Clara slowed down. We would stop—if we were challenged. If we were not, we would proceed at the same slow pace as long as nobody objected. The only illumination at this point came from the large lamps strung along a wire between two posts. They were quite bright, however, and it would be easy for the guards to see that Clara was a woman and that Dick was the man-ape.

I was hoping that the guards would be frozen by surprise for at least a few seconds. And so they were. Dick and Clara did not shout out a warning. But then they knew that I could easily blow both their heads off if they did.

A guard stepped in front of us, calling to us to halt, and

then his eyes widened. Clara opened up with her automatic rifle on her right, as I had directed. I fired with my Bren to my left. Clara got the guard before us and the one on the right. I spun the two other guards around and brought up the fire, hose fashion, across the ground and then up. The officer had jumped up and started to run out through the front of the tent. My bullets caught him in the legs and then the belly.

Nobody at this point was going to stop us, but I wished it had been worked out otherwise. Now the men at the wall that ran from cliffside to cliffside would be alerted. And they could swivel their machine guns and Bofors rapid-fire cannon around to face us and undoubtedly were doing so even now.

And the firing had also alerted the main camp behind us.

I should have sneaked around behind the tent and tried to get the drop on the guards while the jeep, with Clara and Dick, approached them. But I could not do that because I would have put myself in front of the jeep and the fire of Clara and Dick. I might have tried to keep the guards between me and the jeep, but if either Clara or Dick were loyal to the Nine, he or she would have been capable of killing his own men in order to get me.

Clara and Dick got out of the jeep and preceded me into the tent. There were loaded automatic rifles, and bazooka tubes with racks of rockets in the front, and light machine guns on tripods, and hand grenades in the rear. I told Dick and Clara to slip the straps of their rifles over their shoulders so they could take a bazooka and several rockets. I could keep their hands occupied with the tube and the missiles. Dick took the tube. He said he did not know how to operate bazookas, but Clara said she knew all about them.

I attached about ten grenades to hooks on my belt so that all I had to do was to jerk them off to arm them. I yanked the phone wires loose from the short pole behind the tent. We got back into the jeep with me in the back seat again and drove until we were about an eighth of a mile from the wall. We stopped at the bottom of a dip which completely hid us, and Dick and Clara got out ahead of me. Both were sweating heavily with tension, and there was an additional element in Dick's sweat. I could not identify it then, but if I ever smell it again in one of The Folk, I'll know the odor of treachery.

The two searchlights on top of the wall ahead of us were swinging back and forth. No doubt the officer there had phoned into the camp, but they could not tell him anything as yet. When they got to the guard tent, they would know, and they would then switch to wireless.

Dick got down on one knee with the level of the road even with his chest. Clara loaded a rocket in. I fired a burst at both searchlights, and they went out. I shouted, Clara activated the rocket, and, its tail flaming, it arced down the road. It struck dead center and blew the gate apart. Clara immediately loaded and shot another one, this time at the fire-spitting muzzle of the Bofors. Its explosive shells danced across the earth but not directly at us. The rocket struck the wall below the gun emplacement, but it must have killed the crew.

The cannon started shooting again about thirty seconds later. Clara and Dick ducked down to load a third time. I stood up, firing at the dark area immediately around the Bofors until its shells were exploding fifty yards from me, and then I dived for cover.

We were lucky. One shell blew up near the edge of the dip and deafened us and covered us with a spray of dirt and a cloud of smoke. The shell just after it hit the edge behind us at such an angle that it struck a little distance beyond the edge. This explosion showered us, too, and increased our deafness, and, for a moment, numbed us. But I got to my knees, with my Bren pointed at Dick and Clara, and gestured. Even though it was dark, there was enough light from the lamps still operating along the wall for them to make out what I was doing. They got up and loaded and fired, just as the Bofors stopped. There was a heavy fire from two machine guns on one side and one from another—apparently the bazooka had taken out two machine guns, too—and about six automatic rifles.

They were firing blindly, fortunately, and when our fourth and last rocket struck, their fire was momentarily stopped. Clara was a superb bazookist. She placed that rocket just below the Bofors, and it disappeared in a cloud of smoke. We jumped back into the jeep then and roared up out of the dip, headed straight for the shattered gate. Clara fired with her rifle at the machine gun on her side, and I sprayed the left side of the wall. Then I dropped my weapon and threw two grenades in quick succession at the right and the left.

Bullets stitched across the top of the jeep, piercing the hood at an angle from left to right and shattering the glass of the windshield at the extreme upper right-hand side, just missing Clara. It seemed impossible to get through that hellish rain. But the grenades disconcerted them and may have killed or wounded some. Clara's cool firing, I am convinced, stopped several riflemen. Then we were through the gate, the jeep crashing into a piece still standing, and sending us off to one side of the road.

That was a touchy time, because now Clara would be entitled to turn around and fire past me. And she only had to move her rifle a little to cut me in two. But I crouched down so that she had to fire over my head and I could keep watch on her rifle out of the corner of my eye.

It was not as bad as it could have been. By the time the machine gunners could swing around, we were two hundred yards away. Two riflemen sent a stream after us; the tracer bullets spun along the ground as the streams swerved toward us. But our fire stopped them for a moment, and by then we were around a corner of the mountain.

After our first turn onto a higher level of the road, I told Dick to stop the jeep. We listened. Behind us was a roaring as of a dozen vehicles on the road, perhaps a half-mile away. Clara slipped forward and peered over the edge of the road.

"I can see their lights," she said. "There are exactly ten vehicles. Two trucks, the rest are jeeps."

"You two go ahead," I said.

They protested, but I said that I was running this ship. I jumped behind a big boulder on the left-hand side of the road, facing downward, so I could get out of line of the fire of Clara and Dick if they tried anything. But Dick drove off with Clara looking backward.

I ran across the road and down the side, slipping and sliding. I got behind a bush about twelve feet up above the road. And I waited. Presently, the first jeep skidded around the corner of the road, and I jerked a grenade loose and lobbed it into the floor of the jeep. I had one each inside the next two jeeps before the first went off.

The resultant explosions were quite satisfactory. I did not remain to assess the damage until I had gotten to the edge of the road above. By then the mountainside was bright with burning gasoline from the three vehicles. When I looked over, I saw that the road was blocked for some time. The lead vehicle was on its side, the one behind it was catty-cornered across the road, and the third was rammed nose first into it. If the truck behind them had tried to push them off the road, its crew would have been burned to a crisp. I wished they would try it.

However, the men, under the shouted orders of the officers, were climbing up the sides of the mountain to get to my level of the road. I lobbed four of my five remaining grenades down the slope. That apparently killed or wounded many, because the fire from the survivors was feeble. It was strong enough to kill me if I remained, however, so I retreated up the side to the next level. But I was cautious about doing so, since the light from the burning wrecks was enough to illumine me as a dark figure to anybody above.

I still had one grenade, a .38 automatic with a full clip, a knife, and the Bren. The latter probably had very few rounds left. I had just gone behind a large boulder when I heard a muffled sound from above. It could have been Clara. I crouched for a moment and then there was a bellow of outrage and the clatter of a metallic object striking a rock and then slipping and sliding down the slope against other rocks. It sounded to me as if a rifle had been thrown down the mountain, and as if Dick was mad about this.

There were several interpretations I could put on these sounds. But whoever was in trouble would be needing my help. I went on up, though taking advantage of every bit of cover.

As I got closer, I could hear the shuffle of big feet in the earth of the road, pantings, and a woman muttering something. There was a slight swishing, which I interpreted, correctly, as a knife slashing air.

I stuck my head over the edge of the road. In the faint light cast by the fires far below, Dick was an enormous bulk advancing on Clara. He had his hands out ahead of him to grab her, but she was backing away with her knife slicing at him. The jeep, its headlights out, was a few yards up the road.

I stepped out, the Bren pointed at them, and said, "What's going on?"

They stopped. Dick backed away from her.

They both started talking at the same time. I said, "Ladies first. I mean you, Clara."

As usual, my attempt at humor was ignored or misunderstood. Maybe I should reserve them for situations less tense, but I have always thought that tense situations are those that most need humorous relief.

"This traitor, this thing, was going to shoot you!" she said in French. "I hit him over the head and threw the rifle away. He had no other weapon and I only had a knife handy. I couldn't get to my rifle, which is empty anyway, I think. I was trying to keep him away with my knife when you got here."

"That's a lie!" Dick said. "She was the one going to shoot you, when I grabbed the rifle and threw it away."

Dick had spoken in English.

I said, "Since when did you learn French, Dick?"

He stuttered then, and I said, "Why did you feel it necessary to lie to me about that?"

"I didn't lie!" he bellowed. "I can understand some French, even if I can't speak it! I didn't tell you I couldn't understand it!"

If he was innocent, then the omission was trivial, but if he were a loyal agent to the Nine, then this omission was one of a chain of very important facts.

Whatever the truth, I knew now that my caution had not been wasted. One of them was a spy, my enemy. And I could not abandon them to go on my own way because I owed one a debt of gratitude. And the other a debt of revenge. I don't walk away from those who would kill me.

Clara was reluctant, and she reproached me for lacking faith in her. But that was only to relieve her emotions. If she had been in my place she would have done the same, and she knew it. She dropped the knife and backed away so I could pick it up. I had her frisk Dick, and then he frisked her while I watched both. Neither found anything. I put her rifle in the back seat. They got into the front seat with Dick driving again. We went along the road at about fifteen miles, the maximum speed without lights on this narrow winding road.

We had gone about two miles when I saw lights ahead and below. Two vehicles were approaching us from about a mile and a half away. They had to be from the jet strip on the other side of the mountain. I stopped the jeep and watched the lights climb and wind, and then, suddenly, they went out. I returned to the jeep, warily, of course, and said, "Either they've stopped to ambush us or they figure they're getting so close they should turn off the lights. We'll proceed for a mile and then…"

We stopped every hundred yards to listen. Sound carried for miles along that high slope. We could hear shouts from far below us and the motors of the two vehicles approaching us below.

The third time we stopped, we failed to detect the jeeps. After a minute, I concluded they had heard us, and they had stopped to wait. I told Dick to shut the motor off. The slope of the road was steep enough so we could roll on down without pushing. In fact, it was necessary to apply the brake frequently to keep from picking up speed. We went for another half-mile, and then I had the jeep stopped. Our ambushers could hear the brakes from a distance.

I said, "I'm going up the side of the mountain and get above them, Clara. I'll leave your knife here, just in case you are telling the truth. I'm taking your rifle with me, though. You two stay here until I get back. That's an order."

"But he'll kill me!" Clara said.

"She'll knife me!" Dick said.

"I think both of you can take good care of yourselves," I said. "Just stay away from each other."

I went up the slope and left Clara's rifle behind a rock after determining that it had four rounds left in the magazine. It took me about fifteen minutes to work my way up the slope and then down, across the road at a point where Clara and Dick couldn't see me, work down the slope a distance, then along it, and then back up. I came out about thirty feet behind the jeeps we had heard. There were eight men crouching behind them. That left four men at the airstrip, if I had seen all of them when I left the jet.

"They must have seen us," an officer said. "We'll have to send out scouts."

He delegated three men to go ahead. They should fire at the

first suspicious sign. If they ran into an ambush, they should take to the side of the roads.

The three left. I slipped along the slope, crouching, and then stuck my head over the edge. All five were standing together by the hood of the lead jeep. This made things very easy. My only regret was that I had not been in a position to catch all eight. But my grenade went off with a roar two seconds after it landed with a plop in their midst. They froze; they may not even have known what it was, but one of them suspected. He shouted, "Grenade!" and leaped away, but the explosion lifted him and sent him over the edge of the road to my right. He kept on sliding for a long time.

The blast had killed the others, too, and lifted the jeep up and slightly askew in relation to its former position. It had not caught fire but its two right tires and the metal from much of the right side were ripped apart.

The three came running back when they heard the explosion. By then I was up on the slope and I emptied my Bren in a burst that got all three even though they were strung out.

I went down the slope, picked up the rifles and automatics and knives and tossed them into the back seat of the undamaged jeep. I bent over just then fortunately for me. There was a metal box on the floor in the rear which I hoped contained grenades. Four shots sounded in rapid succession from the slope above me and bullets went through the metal of the door and over my head. I dropped flat onto the ground and the last two bullets would have pierced metal and me if I had remained in a crouch.

Then there was a whish of air and a thump as the empty rifle was thrown. It landed behind me in the dirt.

I doubted that Clara had the strength to throw the weapon that far. I doubted that any man except for Caliban and myself, could have cast it that far.

I felt cold then. What had happened to Clara?

"Come on down, you shambling mockery of a man! You ugly stinking ape!" I shouted. "Come on down! I won't shoot you! Use the knife you took from Clara, and I'll use my knife! I want the satisfaction of cutting your big belly open, you missing link! You treacherous beast! Lickling of the Nine!"

There was no answer. He was not going to give his location away. And well for him that he did not, because I had opened the door, removed an automatic rifle and then I let loose at the mountainside. I emptied that magazine and a second and a third, sixty rounds in all.

The echoes died away, the bullets quit ricocheting. There was silence except for a far-off harsh scream of some bird awakened by men's nocturnal activities.

At that moment, I heard the jet. It was high up and, until that moment, had been flying without lights. But they suddenly winked on, flashed, and then swung around. From around the corner of the mountain the light came. The big lamps along the strip had been turned on to guide the jet into the narrow valley.

I jumped into the jeep, turned on the motor, and roared away with a screeching of tires. I headed back up the road because I had to find out what had happened to Clara. I doubted that I had hit Dick. He would have hidden behind one of the many large boulders strewn over the slope. But he was armed with only a knife as far as I knew.

I even turned on the lights so I could go faster. I had gone not more than forty feet when a piece of the night detached itself and leaped from a great rock and landed in the back seat.

He came down in the back instead of on me because I had pressed the accelerator the second I saw him out of the corner of my eye. And I had estimated instantaneously that he would land just behind me. Which is why I rolled out from under the wheel and out of the jeep and onto the ground, leaving the vehicle to conduct itself wherever natural forces led it. If I had stayed there I would not have been able to turn around swiftly enough to defend myself, especially with the wheel cramping me. And he would have struck as soon as his feet hit the back seat.

He bellowed when he realized that I had slipped away. I was only half-aware of it because my head had struck a rock, and I was seeing sprays of light in the night.

If he had bounded out as soon as he had jumped in, he might have had me. But he crouched for a moment while the jeep turned toward the edge of the road. Only when it started to go over did he jump. He landed and rolled like a huge ball, and the vehicle, out of sight, crashed and clanged down the slope and then burst into flames. The glare from below illumined his silhouette, great and broad, long-armed and crest-headed. It also outlined the knife in his hand.

I sat up and groped for the butt of the .38 automatic that should have been sticking out of the holster at my belt. It was not there. I could not think why and then, as my head cleared, I remembered that I had placed it on the seat by me so I could grab it. The only weapon I had was a knife. That would have been enough at one time. I have killed males of The Folk with just a knife. But they were jungle-reared, ignorant of the use of such weapons, ignorant also of such refinements of fighting as judo and karate.

I got to my feet, unstrapped my belt and held the end in my left hand and the knife in my right. Crouching, Dick advanced on me. His knife gleamed dully, reflecting the brightness from below.

In the distance were shouts and, very faintly, the thud of running feet. The men from below were catching up.

From behind me, from around the corner of the mountain, came the thunder of jets as the plane lowered for the final approach.

My head was fully clear now. I stepped toward him and lashed out with the buckle end of the belt. He had not seen what I had behind my back, and so he was surprised. He leaped back, but the buckle hit the end of the knife. He did not lose the knife, but he was not as confident as he had been.

Then I lashed again, and he caught the buckle in his free hand. He was fast, faster than any man I'd ever fought and, of course, stronger than any man whatsoever, including myself. The belt was jerked out of my hand so violently it burned the skin. And it almost carried me into range of his knife.

He came in with a thrust for my belly, which he did not finish. My knife parried his blade and then I stepped back and threw it. It was all-or-none in this case. If he blocked it, he had me.

The knife sank into his paunch.

His own knife dropped. He staggered back, clutching at the hilt. Then he fell on his back, and air rattled in his throat.

Rifles exploded down the road. Bullets whizzed by me. Others raced along the dirt, just missing me. I had not time to pull my knife from Dick. I should have taken the time, have risked the bullets. If I had pulled that knife out... but I didn't, and what is done is done.

To have gone down the slope was to put myself in the twilight illumination from the burning jeep. I leaped across the road and was up the slope and crawling among the rocks. The men probed the slope with heavy firepower. However, they had seen me only at a distance and unclearly, and they had no idea where I was on the mountainside. They concentrated most of their fire on the area behind me, since they assumed that I would be traveling away from them. Then they quit, probably because they were running short of ammunition.

I went back down the road on a course about fifty yards parallel with it. There were no men where I wanted to cut down the slope to the lower level where I had left Clara, so I went swiftly there. The jeep was still standing where I'd left it. I did not understand why the pursuers had not used it. By it stood a single man with a rifle. On the road at his feet was a form. It was too dim there to see well, but I smelled her. She was still alive.

It was easy to come up behind the guard and break his neck. Once more, I was armed with rifle, pistol, and a knife.

Clara was bound hand and foot and gagged with strips torn from her shirt. Dick had taken her alive and tied her up so that she could pay properly for her defection. I untied and ungagged her.

"Can you climb up the hill?" I said.

She cleared her throat and said, "Yes. How in the world did you get away from them? And Dick?"

"He's dead. What's the matter with the jeep?"

"I don't know. The bullets must have damaged it somewhere.

When the men came, they tried to start it, but the motor wouldn't even turn over."

I could not have used it anyway. I picked up a bag of canned food and two containers of water. I gave her a rifle and two magazines from the jeep's floor.

We started up over the mountain. A few minutes later, the sky grayed. We increased our pace. Within an hour, we were still going strong, though she was panting. Far below us, two jeeps carrying armed men stopped by the men who had been pursuing us. The jeeps evidently came from the airstrip on the other side of the mountain. They were too far away for me to identify the newcomers. So far, the jet had not taken off.

Crouching behind a rock, I watched the long conference. Occasionally, an officer turned his binoculars up the slope and swept the terrain. None stopped with me in their line of sight. Then the jeeps started toward the valley. If any of the Nine were in the jeeps, the men in charge at the camp would be lucky to get off alive. The Nine would never forgive them.

There was no more smoke from any of the burning vehicles. The roads were clear now, and jeeps full of armed men were coming up the roads. I counted eight. These were almost bumper to bumper as they raced along the dry earth, throwing up large clouds of dust. Then they pulled over to the extreme edge, the wheels on the rim of the dropoff, to let the jeeps from the airstrip by. As soon as these had passed, the jeeps resumed their dangerous speed. I had assumed that the men in them were out to hunt me down, but the vehicles continued on around the mountain. Perhaps they were going to come up from the other side to cut me off.

They did not have enough men for that to adequately cover the area. If they had had a copter, they might have done it.

When we got to the top of the mountain, I saw what they were doing. The jeeps, so far away they were almost invisible, were parked near the two-motored passenger jet. Evidently the newcomers intended to leave soon, and they wanted to make sure I did not attack them at the plane or try to steal it.

We went on down the mountain and by late afternoon were near the bottom. The sun flashed frequently off the binoculars directed toward our slope. But if they saw us, they made no move. And I did not believe they would not come after us if they did see us.

Clara said, "Why are we heading straight toward them?"

"They don't expect us to do so," I said. "At least, I don't think they will. I'll admit I've been very aggressive, but that was because I was trying to escape. I want to get as close as possible because I suspect that one or more of the Nine came in on that plane. And it's obvious the plane is waiting to take them away again. Also, if we get a chance to steal the plane, we will."

Clara kissed me and said, "You're wonderful! A real Tarzan! A beautiful *Starkathr*! My loveable black-haired, gray-eyed *Übermensch*! Samson and Hercules and Odysseus rolled into one! Nobody but you could have gotten out of that canyon, and anybody else would have left us there! And then to get away and kill so many of them! And then to attack them when we could get away!"

"I *have* been pushing my luck these last few days," I said.

For some reason, she thought that was funny. She choked trying to repress her laughter.

Halfway down, we were forced to dive for the shelter of a large boulder. Mortar shells began exploding below us. We clung to the rock, our faces pressed into the hard ground, while at least thirty-five shells roared along the face of the mountain. The closest, however, was about forty yards below us. That was close enough, but, except for shaken nerves and insulted eardrums, we were not hurt.

After waiting for five minutes after the last of the shells, I looked out over the boulder. The tiny figures were engaged in doing something, but they were not attending the mortars, which glittered in the sun just before the shadows of the western mountain fell on them. Nor was there any movement toward us. I decided that they had lobbed the shells just to scare us out if we were anywhere in the neighborhood.

We stayed behind the boulder for another fifteen minutes and then started our descent again. By the time we were three-quarters of the way down, the shadows from the other mountain had fallen on us. We kept going in the twilight. When we were about a quarter-mile from the jet strip, we stopped to eat cold food from our cans.

Just before we finished the meal, a helicopter chuttered around the side of the mountain to the west. The lights along the strip flashed on, but the machine continued on over us and disappeared. There was no longer a lack of choppers. This one was going to pick up the newcomers and bring them to the jet, I was sure of that. That would avoid bringing them on the road in jeeps and so open to ambush from me.

Moreover, when daylight came, the chopper would undoubtedly be out looking for us. And other choppers might be on the way to aid in the hunt.

When night was fully alive, I left Clara behind a boulder near the foot of the mountain. The lights were on along the strip and around the four tents. I couldn't see them, but I had no doubt that mass-detection buttons were strung around the perimeters of the camp and the jet. Four men had just finished erecting a metal structure about thirty feet high on the tip of which was an antenna array. A minute later, the array began rotating. I stayed behind a bush. It looked as if it was a personnel detector, either radar or a heat-sensitive device. It must have been brought in by the jet. When detectors exist which can distinguish between the gait of a man or a woman at a range of twelve miles, the skulker at night has to be exceedingly careful and crafty. Clara and I had been lucky coming down the mountainside. If the detector had been installed then, we would not have been able to get away from the helicopter.

I watched for a while and determined that there were thirty-six men in all. Half were stationed as guards outside the camp and around the plane. The rest were cooking or lying down on sleeping bags on the ground or were doing something in the tents. I could smell their tension, and the infrequent but sharp laughter verified my nose.

There were two 60mm mortars with piles of about sixty shells apiece. There were six .50 caliber machine guns along the perimeter of a circle described around the jet and the camp. Every man carried an automatic rifle. The jeeps were parked inside along the perimeter so that the men could fire from behind them.

The logical place for the choppers to land would be close to the jet so that the passengers could be transferred with the least exposure.

I crawled back to Clara, taking a long time because I had to keep behind boulders or in depressions as much as possible and when I could not I moved only when the antenna was turned away from me.

"The chopper will be coming back on one of two routes," I said. "Either all the way around the mountain, along the shoulder. Or directly over it, the shorter route. They know we have an M-15, so they will be flying high, either way. But maybe they won't be too high. They must figure that we won't be dumb enough to hang around here once our escape route was open. Especially since the chopper came. But they also must figure that they can't rely on me not to be dumb. Their experience must have convinced them that I don't always run."

She chuckled and kissed my cheek and said, "I think they don't know what to think."

I told her what I wanted her to do, if she wished to cooperate. If she didn't, she must leave. I did not want her around unless I knew exactly where she was and what she was supposed to do. She agreed, without hesitation, to obey me.

Even so, she was reluctant to part with me. She kissed me again, and she said she hoped she'd see me again. But she was happy, even if somewhat scared. She was out of what had seemed a hopeless situation, and she might yet get out of this one.

It would take most of the night for her to get stationed, since she had to go back over the mountain and then around to a place along the shoulder. I crawled back down to a position about a quarter-mile from the camp. If the chopper did come directly over the mountain, it would start lowering close enough for me to get it in my range. Of course, I would have to get the hell out immediately because the combined firepower would be directed at me.

The chance of getting the chopper was about a hundred to one, and the chance of getting away alive was about a thousand to one.

If the enemy had been anybody but one of the Nine, I would not have risked it. But I hated them so that I was willing to take the risk. Clara was out of range of fire from the camp, so that if she got the copter, she could get away.

The night fell to pieces, and the sun came up again. I had suspected that the chopper would carry the newcomers by day. It would be easier to spot us then, and it was also safer for the jet to take off. About a half hour after dawn, I heard the chutter of the machine. It was much lower than I had expected, about five hundred feet up. But it did not fly directly in a straight line. It zigzagged, and at first I thought it was taking evasive action. Then it came to me that this might be a dry run. It was not carrying VIPs; it held armed men. They were trying to fool us into exposing our positions by firing at them. Then, after dealing with us, they would go back for their passengers.

Trust the Nine to be supercautious!

I got under the overhang of the huge boulder and lay still. The machine passed almost directly overhead. It went as far as the camp and then it returned, but further to the north. It disappeared over the mountain. I suspected that it would come back again, this time around the shoulder, near where Clara was. I hoped she would not fire, that she would figure out that this was a dry run.

There was nothing to do except wait. The bulk of the mountain deadened any sound on the other side. I could not get up and climb to the top, because of the personnel radar. Therefore, wait it would be. My patience is great; I learned it in a hard school when I was young, hunting for meat. But this was the most painful watch I had ever put in.

An hour passed. Then the chopper came over the top, and this time it was even lower. Obviously, it was making another sweep, daring us to shoot. If we were lucky enough to bring it down, the Nine would have lost another helicopter and some servants, but they could then use the jeep to get to the jet. Or they could wait until another helicopter arrived. After ten thousand or so years, they had developed the ability to take the greatest of pains and to use as much time as needed.

I was certain that one of the Nine had to be involved. This much trouble would not have been taken for anyone lesser, not even for an important candidate for the empty seat.

It was not enough for the machine to be taken over this mountain. It went over the camp to the mountain on the opposite side and cruised up and down and back and forth for an hour. It seemed to be about only two hundred feet above the surface.

Then it rose straight up and flew back over my mountain maintaining several thousand feet height above ground level.

By then I decided that I had been wasting my time. I had taken a long shot and should have known better.

I waited. And I waited. The sun sank behind the western range. The camp showed no unusual activity. Several jeeps, which had left at noon, returned before dusk. These carried only the men who had left earlier and two bazookas and bazooka rockets.

I crawled to the top of the mountain and descended much more swiftly on the other side. I knew where Clara was and so called out softly to her and then waited for the counter-word. The wind was carrying the scent to me, and so I knew that she was alone.

"I don't know what he's doing," I said. She understood by *he* that I meant one or more of the Nine. "I'm sure he's inside the caves and probably sending out all sorts of messages. There must be a powerful short-wave set in there. I don't know when he's coming out, but you can be sure that we'll never get close enough to get the chopper that carries him unless we want to commit suicide."

"Perhaps it's too big a job for just us two," she said hopefully. "We can run away and fight again another day."

"We'll try one more day," I said. "If nothing happens we leave tomorrow night."

Part of that night we spent working our way down the mountain to the end of the valley into which the jet had flown. We approached the end of the strip by a shallow ravine. This lay about a hundred yards beyond the rammed earth of the end of the strip. Behind us was rough land with sparse bush for two hundred yards, and then a mountain began to curve gently up. The jet had to swing down over its two thousand foot height and come down close to the surface if it was to settle its wheels at this end. The strip was long enough to take the two-jet type but not a four-jet.

The personnel radar on top of the tower at the north end of the strip was undoubtedly able to detect us. And at this distance we would not have been able to see it if the lights had not been turned on. We crawled along out of the ravine until we were past the foot of the mountain on our right and out of the radar's line of sight.

I told Clara what I intended to do. She said that it sounded forlorn and, indeed, suicidal. I agreed and said I would try it, anyway.

The rest of the night we slept peacefully, except once, when I awoke and thought I had heard a leopard. But the scream was so far off, and I got in on the very end of it, so I could not be sure. If there were leopards here, they would not be man-eaters. I went back to sleep.

At dawn we ate the last of our food and drank the last of our water. An hour later, I heard the chopper. It rose high over the mountain and came down vertically exactly over the camp. The figures that got out of the machine were tiny, of course, because we were so far away. We were behind a rock at an angle to the camp, looking past the shoulder of the mountain west of the camp. But one of the figures was so bulky and long-armed and crest-skulled, it had to be Dick. I had not killed him after all. The knife must not have gone in as deeply as I had thought. And he may have been pretending to be dead so that I would approach to pull the knife out, and he could take me by surprise. He might well have done so, if those riflemen had not run me away. He was walking without any help, so he must have been quickly patched up. Caliban's medical inventions had long been of great service to the organization of the Nine.

The second figure that magnetized my attention was that of a broad-framed, black-skinned, white-haired man. His walk, distinctive even at that distance, identified him as Mubaniga.

The third figure was a tall skinny bald-headed man who could be none other than Doctor Murtagh.

For some reason, he had been called back from his journey to Germany.

Mubaniga got into the jet with a number of armed men. Dick and Murtagh remained on the ground. I knew then they had been left behind to hunt for us. Murtagh had been recalled to complete a job that he had erred in marking off. He undoubtedly would have liked to tell Mubaniga that I should have been executed the moment I was captured, but he would not have dared.

Two jeeps rode out along each side of the jet. At the end of the strip, they stopped, and the five occupants of each got out. They advanced with rifles ready and investigated the terrain for several hundred yards in each direction. Two men took stations on the edge of the ravine and faced outward. The others formed two lines near the end of the strip.

The jet took a long time warming up. I ducked down into the ravine at a point where it curved and so kept me from being seen by the two guards. My moves were dictated then solely by my hearing. I crouched there with the rifle in hand, the .45 in its holster, and the knife in its sheath.

Clara Aekjaer was in a hole beneath the overhang of a boulder set on the hillside but out of line of the personnel radar. She had her orders to come out when she saw me running.

The twin jets roared, but the pilot was still testing them. Then I heard something unexpected. The copter was swinging across the strip. I do not know why I had overlooked it in my plans. I suppose because I had regarded it solely as a carrier in the last stage of getting the jet away with its important passenger.

But it was coming down the strip now and would then go up and down the gently sloping mountain to make doubly sure that no one was hidden there.

I shoved myself against the bank and tried to look like a rock. My skin was smeared with dirt, and my clothes were covered with clay, so I probably did look like a rock. And there was a projection above me to throw me into the shade.

The copter flew over about a hundred yards ahead of me. I dared to turn my head slowly to look over the opposite side of the ravine. The big chopper was zigzagging at only fifty feet above the ground. Its sides bristled with machine guns and rifles. It proceeded for about half a mile and then, its occupants believing that anybody beyond that could not harm the jet because it would be too high then, returned. It was on its way to land when the change in the noise of the jet showed that the plane was taking off.

That was my starting gun.

I ran down the rocky bed of the ravine, but I was still crouched over. Clara should have started to crawl out of the hole the moment she saw me go. She would get out just far enough to shoot down the nearest guard.

He, fortunately, had not resisted the temptation to turn and look at the jet for just a moment. Perhaps he wanted to reassure himself that he was not in its direct path. I had not been counting on him to do that, but it helped. It gave me a few more seconds to get down the ravine before I had to slow down and start shooting at the guard at the far end.

The copter was still coming down and its vanes, plus the roar of the jets, helped drown out Clara's fire.

The guard nearest me turned his head, saw me, froze, and then he crumpled to one side, dropped his rifle, and slid out over the ravine. He fell in front of me. I leaped over him, swinging my rifle up to point at the other guard, who had just become aware that his comrade had fallen. But he fell, too, hit by Clara's fire.

Halfway between the two corpses, I stopped. I listened and then, visualizing just how far down the strip the jet was, I bent down, gathered my leg muscles, and leaped to the top of the ravine, six feet up, and over it. My rifle was spitting as I came up and I caught every man on the right end of the strip. The burst stitched them together in death.

That they were facing outward and away from me helped the surprise.

The man at the nearest end of the line on my left side had seen the first guard fall. He had started to fire without warning the man on his right. This man, however, had heard the gun shooting even above the noises of the two craft. He had started shooting in Clara's direction, and then the others heard and began firing.

Clara's fire and mine were like two hoses started at each end, and they met in the middle.

The pilot of the jet must have seen what was happening. It was too late for him to stop. He could do nothing except try to get past us.

I crouched, Clara continued to fire at the oncoming plane. It lifted, perhaps prematurely in an effort to escape our bullets. I don't know. But I raised up and threw the rifle so that it spun once and then the barrel went straight into the plane's port jet.

I had not time to throw myself down. The wing shot a few

inches above my head, and I was deafened by the roar.

Theoretically, the jet could fly with one engine dead. But things happened too fast. The rifle had wrecked the engine, the pilot had lifted the plane a trifle too early, and, for all I know, Clara's bullets had hit someone or something vital.

The jet plowed into the side of the mountain behind us and blew up. Pieces of metal spun through the air and fell around us. Fire shot up, and black smoke poured out a hundred feet high.

The people at the other end of the strip were paralyzed. I had banked on this. I leaned down, took Clara's hand and pulled her up onto the ground so swiftly that she cried out with pain. We ran to the nearest jeep. Clara got into the driver's seat and started the motor. By then the people in the copter had recovered some of their senses. It started to lift off, turned, and a machine gun and a rifle in its starboard bay began to shoot fire. And the men on the ground were piling into the jeeps there. In the first jeep were Dick and Murtagh.

If they had had any time to reflect, they would have fled without paying any attention to us. They had allowed one of the Nine to be killed, and their own lives were forfeit. Murtagh's candidacy was automatically canceled, and he was as much the quarry of the Nine as I.

But they reacted with their reflexes only. They were still carrying out the Nine's orders, and they intended to kill the man who had thwarted them so much.

Clara wheeled the jeep around with tires screeching and headed toward the copter. He spun the copter around and started away, then stopped it and started back toward us. The fire from the gunners dug up the dirt on all sides of us and a few bullets pierced the hood. But Clara drove the jeep as if it were a bull with a nest of hornets hung under its tail. It swerved this way and that so violently that I had to jam my feet against the back of the seat in front of me and my back against the seat behind me. I fired as steadily as I could, and then the chopper veered away on its side and crashed in the path of the oncoming jeeps. It blew up, spraying flaming gasoline everywhere. Clara jammed on the brakes just in time to keep us from slamming into the inferno. She backed up quickly enough while our faces seared, turned around, and raced off.

The other jeeps backed up and went around the flames, and then the chopper exploded again. Presumably, it was the overheated ammunition. Fire like surf shot out and covered some of the jeeps. Men jumped out of the nearest vehicle while it was still going and rolled screaming on the ground.

Murtagh's jeep was partly splashed, but he and Dick got away. I shot at them but did not think I hit them.

Those behind, however, were occupied by determined men. They came around the flames and pursued us as if they had learned nothing from the past few minutes, not to mention the previous three days. And perhaps they were right in refusing to learn, since my good fortune could not last forever.

Clara took the jeep along the edge of the ravine, cut across its end, and we were loose on very rough country. We bounced high and hard, so violently that all I could do was hang on. But those behind us could not shoot either. Our course was strictly dictated by the terrain, which was as wrinkled as the face of a centenarian. The jeep cut back and forth, leaped out from the edge of ridges and slammed into the ground with bone-cracking and muscle-snapping force. Once she tried to stop the vehicle in time to keep it from going over another ravine, which was too broad for us to traverse. The jeep skidded toward the edge, stopped, teetered, and then went over on its side. Clara leaped out one way and I the other. I jumped up at once and looked down, expecting to see her crushed underneath the vehicle. But she was on its other side, flat against the earth. The jeep lay on its side.

I jumped down, picked her up, said, "Are you all right?"

She was white-faced, but she nodded. I handed her a rifle and said, "Keep them off while I fix this!"

"How can you fix that?" she said, but she moved on down the ravine and stood on top of a rock so she could fire over the edge.

I crouched down, got a good grip on the jeep, and slowly straightened up. The jeep, groaning, came up, I almost slipped, but not quite, and the jeep was upright.

Clara started shooting then. I ran up to her, tapped her shoulder, she turned, started, and then grinned. Some of the color was returning. The racket of gunfire and the gouting of earth along the edge of the ravine was still going on when we drove off along the bed of the cut. We did not go swiftly or too far. About three hundred yards down, we were stopped by a dropoff of about twenty feet. She drove the vehicle over, abandoning it just before it reached the lip of the little cliff. I had hoped that the jeep might survive the fall. But it dived into the dirt nose first, and the sturdy radiator, which had suffered so much, finally broke. Water pooled out from it.

Even so, we had a good headstart on the others. They were very cautious about approaching long after our fire had ceased. The steep ridge which had caused Clara to skid the jeep prevented their vehicles from going any further unless they went far to the north. They did follow us on foot, however, because I saw them coming out of the ravine when we were about five hundred feet up a mountain. This was partially covered with bush and trees. The rain forest would start just on the other side of this mountain, and the only one who could track us then would be Dick.

If he had been raised by The Folk, he would have been somebody to fear. His nose was keener than mine, but he had been raised by humans who lived on the edge of the rain forest but seldom went into it. He would be lost. And he could not travel as swiftly as Clara and I. He had too much weight to carry, and his legs were too short.

I kept on going with Clara panting heavily and having to stop now and then. The gap remained between us and the pursuers. But when, at evening, we plunged through the dense rim-growth into the cool and dark mansions of the rain forest, I stopped.

After getting Clara up into a tree, I returned to the tanglery by the border between bush and forest. From a branch a hundred and fifty feet high, I watched the tiny figures toil up the hill. They were lost from time to time in the bush, and then, as dusk fell, they became invisible.

I had discarded one rifle when it ran out of ammunition. The other was with Clara, and it held only six rounds. I carried the .45 automatic and my knife. I was tired. I would have liked to hole up for the night. Clara and I had satisfied our thirst at a pothole and filled our canteens. She had eaten nothing since breakfast, and I had had only a small golden mouse I caught by the tail while I was on my way out.

But I had a job to finish.

I climbed down and went through the bush, though very cautiously. Dick's keen ears and nose made him worth all the others put together in the jungle, and I did not want to stumble over him lying in ambush.

About a hundred yards away, I heard a very strange noise. They were all chanting my name.

"Lord Grandrith! Lord Grandrith!"

If it was a trick, and I did not know what else it could be, it was unique. It also whetted my curiosity to the point where I could not have stayed away.

At the last, I climbed a tree and peered down through the branches of two trees ahead of me at the camp.

They were cooking over Caliban's lightweight stoves. Eight of the ten were shouting out my name together. Dick squatted by the stove, his voice booming above the others. Murtagh stood in the center of the small open area with his hands held out.

I called out from behind the trunk during a pause in their chanting. "What do you want?"

Murtagh shouted back, "We want to parley with you."

"Why?"

"I think you know why. We failed, and so the Nine will kill us. We would like to team up with you. Some of us now believe that you and Caliban might actually have a chance against the Nine. And we have talents that you can use, since you can use every bit of help you can get, despite your fantastic success so far!"

"Throw your weapons into the bush! All of them! Knives and derringers, too, if you have them!"

They were reluctant to do so but only because they felt naked without them. And they could not be sure that I would not then mow them down.

When the last weapons, which did include two derringers, were tossed over a bush, I dropped from branch to branch, fell twelve feet to the ground, and then walked into the clearing. My pistol and knife were in their sheaths.

Murtagh was smiling now. I did not like him trying to be friendly any more than I had when he was trying to kill me. But alliances in wartime are not based on likes or dislikes. When he started to speak, I held up my hand.

"If you are to join me," I said, "you must make it worth my while to accept you. I need much information. What do you know about my wife? And what is the situation in regard to Caliban?"

"I am a candidate," he said, "but that does not mean I am fully in the confidence of the Nine. You know that. I have heard nothing at all about your wife. I do not even know the name of the man who is in charge of the business of getting her. As for Caliban, well, I was ordered to Germany to track him down after I had put you away in the canyon. I was told that he had been seen in the vicinity of Gramzdorf, a village and a castle in the Black Forest. I was told that he had been trying to kill Iwaldi. I was also told that we were to kill Iwaldi, if we got a chance, and…"

The world was certainly turning topsy-turvy. Here I was discussing an alliance with men who had been trying their best to kill me. And here I was being told that the Nine were trying to kill one of their own—old Iwaldi, the wrinkled dwarf whose white beard fell to his waist.

Joining forces with hated enemies was, of course, nothing new for mankind. Or even for me. I killed a number of Germans in East Africa during World War I, not for patriotism but for personal revenge. Then I found out that the atrocities that had set me on the blood trail were the work of a small band of criminals in the East African German forces. They would have been shot by their commander if he had known what they had done. Later, I became very good friends with Colonel Paul von Lettow-Vorbeck, who kept two hundred thousand British troops at bay with just eleven thousand men, most of them black Africans. Of course, anyone reading the volume of my biography dealing with this phase of my life would get the mistaken notion that it was the Germans whose hordes would have overwhelmed the British if it had not been for me. But my biographer was always more interested in dramatic values than in facts, and he was full of the intense anti-German feeling of that time. The truth is that von Lettow-Vorbeck was a greater guerrilla leader than Lawrence of Arabia, but he did not get any publicity. Besides, he was on the defeated side.

I doubted that there was anything admirable about the reptilian Murtagh to make me respect him as I had von Lettow-Vorbeck. But he was highly intelligent and ruthless, and he could be used, even if never fully trusted.

He said, "I was on my way to Germany when I got a message saying that I should go to Paris instead. Caliban had disappeared there. And then I got another message telling me to return. You had escaped. I couldn't believe it, but I had to. I met Mubaniga at a strip in the Congo, and we came here. He put me in charge of killing you, and then he took off, as you know. He did not say where he was going. But I got hold of a message which indicated that he would be going to Salisbury, England. Why, I don't know."

I smiled. If he was able to read an intercepted message, which he had no business doing, he had learned how to translate the language the Nine used among themselves. I have no idea what this language is or how ancient. But I got hold of a number of papers while I was the Speaker for the Nine during an annual ceremony, and I learned how to interpret that language, too. I surmised that Murtagh, when he was the Speaker, had done the same. He was a brave man or a foolhardy one to take that chance.

The language itself, as a side comment, seems to be distantly related to Basque. It is my guess that it was the original tongue of Anana, the terrible old woman who is chieftainess of the Nine. It is probably one of a superfamily that extended around the Mediterranean and possibly over much of Europe, before the Indo-Hittite speakers came out of the forests of what is today middle Germany.

"Where is this strip in the Congo?" I said. "Does it have a short-wave set that can reach Europe? Can we get there swiftly on foot? Or do we have to steal a copter or plane?"

He reached slowly into his jacket and pulled out a map. He unfolded it on the ground in the beam of a flashlight.

"It's there, in the Ituri forest," he said.

The map was French, and his finger hovered above a cross made of red ink in an area marked *Pygmées*.

It was about eighty miles from where we were. I could make

it on foot in twenty-four hours if I knew exactly where it was. But if I let the others accompany me, I would take anywhere from six to eight days. I needed them. At least, I needed Murtagh, and I did not want to abandon Clara. Once we got to civilization, she could do what she wanted to do. But I had to get her out of the wilderness because I owed it to her.

"Are any more planes coming in to the strip back there?" I said, indicating the area outside the caves.

"Several choppers, at least," Murtagh said. "They should be there now or coming in very soon. Oh, you have cost the Nine dearly!"

"Not as dearly as I plan," I said. "Wait here. I'll be back within twenty minutes."

I returned with Clara Aekjaer. While we ate, we went over my campaign. Murtagh tried to overrule me several times; he could not give up the idea that he was the leader. But I put him in his place without humiliating him, and after a while he saw that he could not push me around in any way. On the other hand, I did accept several suggestions of his for improving our plans.

Late at night, we all bedded down. I could have retired into the forest with Clara to make sure we weren't jumped on while we slept. But it was a case of full acceptance of partnership or none at all. I was ready to dissolve the alliance the moment I saw signs of treachery. Until then, I could not treat them as leopards ready to turn on me.

Even so, I had trouble getting to sleep. Perhaps it was Dick that kept my brain occupied. I did not know what to do with him. We could not take him to England with us. Even if we had shaved and clothed him and pulled his long canines, he still would have attracted attention we could not tolerate for one minute. I could have left him in the forest, but, as I said, he had been raised as a human, not as one of The Folk, and he would starve or go crazy from loneliness.

If I had had time, I could have gone into the wilderness with him, taught him how to hunt, how to build a nest against the rain and the cold. And the female I had seen last year might still be roaming the mountains in Uganda. We could find her and Dick could take her as his mate. And they could have young, and The Folk might not die out.

But that was a fantasy. Dick's tastes in food were set. He could not adapt to a diet of juicy white grubs, rodents, birds' eggs, raw birds, wild nuts and berries, and an occasional piece of meat, not always fresh by any means. In the wet and often chilly rain forest of the mountains, he would probably suffer from colds and he would likely die of pneumonia. He could migrate to the rain forest of the Gabon lowlands, but I doubted that he would get the female to go there with him, even if he could find and successfully woo her.

Besides, as I had found out when in the box canyon, Dick desired human females because he had been raised as a human. He probably would have thought the female of The Folk to be as ugly as a human thinks a gorilla is.

I told myself that I had no cause to worry about him. Though he had tried to kill me while pretending to be my friend, that was only something anybody would do to gain an advantage in war, and I did not hold it against him.

Then I fell into a fit of nostalgia. Suddenly, I wanted to shuck off this kind of life. I was tired, sick even, of killing and of being on the run or the attack. I wanted to get away from all these humans, and the subhuman, and travel deep into the forest. I wanted to go naked and hunt the pig and the antelope with only a knife. I wanted to sleep in a cozy nest in the trees, hear only the muted noise of the animals of the closed-canopy forest, be in the shadow and the silence. I did not want to see another human being for... for a long long time. I wanted to be free with an obligation only to myself. I could commune with the beasts, with Natu. , as Whitman expresses it in several of his poems. I hated civilization, especially the big cities, especially London with its wet chilly air and coughs and sneezes and running noses, its blare and screech and roar, its citizens bumping into each other, the grit and rasp of hatred and madness fouling its air along with the physical poisons.

If it had not been for my wife, and for Caliban, I would have risen then and walked into the forest and left them to work out their own problems. As long as the Nine left me alone, I would not have bothered them, would not even have thought of them.

But Clio might be in danger. And Caliban, once my most dangerous enemy, was now my best friend.

I sighed deeply, turned over, and managed to fold in the night over my brain.

In the morning, Dick asked me if he could go with us to London. I told him why that was impossible. He finally admitted that all the logic was on my side. But he asked what he could do then. I replied that he should return to his foster parents, who lived in a hut near the edge of the rain forest. The time would come when Caliban and I would be ready to attack the Nine in the caves. Then we would need him, since he was a truly formidable antagonist. He grimaced and touched the bandage just above his navel. The next time someone came at him with a knife, and he himself had only a knife, he would throw it. He was not going to get tricked again.

My knife had not gone deeply because he had grabbed it even as it struck. He had cut his hands, too, but the pseudo-skin which Caliban had devised for wounds had been applied to the cuts. The knife wound had had to be glued after repairs were made, again with the use of one of Caliban's medical inventions. Dick could not exert himself fully yet without fear of tearing the wound open. The ride on the jeep when I was being chased had caused him considerable pain. But he would be completely healed within a week unless something broke open the wound.

Dick nodded when I said that they also served who waited. But he scowled, and that was a fearsome sight. The bulging bones above the sunken russet eyes, the blue-black skin, the protruding jaws with the long sharp yellow canines, all these looked fierce enough when he was smiling. On the way back to the jet strip, he was silent, except when addressed, and then he was curt and surly.

The first thing Murtagh did when we reached the jeeps was to report over the radio to the camp. The operator at the receiving end could not conceal his astonishment. He had supposed, along with everybody else, that Murtagh had either been killed when he took off after me or else had kept on going to put as much distance between himself and the Nine as he could.

"I have taken Lord Grandrith prisoner, and I am bringing him in," Murtagh said to the officer who had been summoned. "I also have the countess, Clara Aekjaer, prisoner."

The officer, a man named ibn Khalim, was flabbergasted.

Part of his reaction was because I had been taken alive. But the other part, which he would not admit if he had been asked, was amazement that Murtagh thought he would be forgiven now that he had me in custody. That he should have allowed Mubaniga, one of the Nine, to be killed was unforgivable. But if Murtagh was stupid enough to come back, so much the better.

Ibn Khalim quit talking for a moment, apparently to consult a higher authority. Then he ordered Murtagh to come in immediately. Clara and I were to be brought in alive. This was the personal order of Anana herself, relayed by radio from somewhere in Europe.

The ancient woman must have splendid things in mind for me. She might even be planning to save me for the annual ceremonies, when I could be tortured as an object lesson for the candidates. I could imagine her anger. And I smiled, though smiling at the thought of her is like being amused by the thought of Death Herself. If things worked out as I planned, she was going to be even angrier.

The journey back was much slower and more comfortable than that out. I sat in the front seat of the land jeep with two rifles at my head and my legs and arms seemingly tied together. Clara sat in the front seat of the second jeep, also seemingly bound. About a half-mile from the strip, a chopper met us. It flew about fifty feet above us all the way to the strip.

The mass of armed men I had expected to be waiting for us at the strip was not there. There were twenty men altogether, and six of these were stationed at the strip at all times. The others had come up by jeep from the big camp around the mountain. This small a number could mean that Murtagh and his men were to be treated as conquering heroes, so they would be put off their guard. Once Clara and I were turned over to the soldiers, Murtagh and his men would be separated. And then, dispersed, each would be arrested.

This would be a much less bloody way than attacking them while they were armed and organized. The Nine had lost so heavily that they were taking the subtle way.

This was more than I expected, especially since we had no plans for going deeper than the strip. We were prepared to open fire on whatever number of men was lined up to receive us. If we jumped the gun, we might be able to bull our way through. Now the task was so much easier.

The chopper settled down just as we drove up. An officer strode forward to greet Murtagh, who got out of the jeep and shot the officer through the chest.

We lost two dead and one wounded. But most of the others were cut down before they could bring their rifles into action.

I flew one chopper and Murtagh the other. We took off as soon as our men had climbed in and we had determined that we had enough fuel. We kept close to the tops of the forest once we got past the mountains, and we came into the strip in the middle of the Ituri forest with our wheels almost touching the treetops. There were one four-motored jet and two choppers near the small camp. The fighting was brief and bloody, and the four survivors ran into the jungle rather than surrender. We let them go.

While Murtagh was warming up the jet, and his men were placing dynamite to blow up the camp and the choppers, I sent a message to my men in Dakar. I did not expect to receive any acknowledgement, since Murtagh told me he assumed that my men had been located and killed. But they were a mobile unit—how mobile I won't reveal because I will be using them again. And they answered.

It was true that I had revealed the code to Murtagh under the influence of his drug. But, as I said, a questioner isn't going to get everything he should know unless he asks the right questions. Murtagh did not ask me if there was more than one code. He got the code for the particular day he questioned me. The Nine had transmitted a message on the following day, and so they had used the wrong code. My men had answered, given misleading information, and then had moved on.

Today was Wednesday, and so I transmitted the proper code for that day. I outlined what had happened, told them what I needed and how soon I'd be there. And then I asked if they had heard anything about my wife or from Caliban.

They knew nothing of Clio. But they had a reply to my first message sent some days ago.

It was from Doc Caliban. He was leaving for the county of Wiltshire in southern England. His ultimate destination was Stonehenge, the ancient ruins about seven and a half miles north of Salisbury. I was to get there as quickly as possible unless I considered events in Africa to have taken a very important turn. He was hot on the track of Iwaldi, and the business at hand might mean the end of the world—in a sense.

The message had been sent the day before.

If that proud and almost neurotically self-sufficient man was asking me for help, he must be in very hot waters indeed.

I sent him a message which I did not think he would get until it was too late, if he ever received it. Then I ran out of the station and signaled the others to get into the plane. Dick stopped me. He bellowed at me against the roar of the jets.

"Can't you take me with you? I could be of great help. Do you know anybody who has my strength?"

I shook my head and shouted back, "I'm sorry, I really am! But you can be of far more value to us if you stay here! When the time comes to go into the caves, we'll need you very much! And we just can't take you with us! You'd attract attention, which is the last thing we can stand! You might cause us to be killed by your very presence!"

"Then go to hell!" he bellowed, his throat sac swelling, and by that I knew he was almost insanely furious.

Logic told me to shoot him then and there, because there was no telling what he might do to hurt us. We could not afford to take the least chance. But I did not follow logic, of course, since I just could not kill him without adequate provocation. I even yelled at him to get into the jungle before the explosions.

Then I got into the plane, and the port was closed, we took off, and, as we swung back around, I pressed the button that transmitted a frequency to sets below. The two choppers and the tents blew up in a great cloud.

When the Nine heard of this, they would be doubly enraged, if that was possible. Never had they been so threatened, so outraged, so thumb-at-nosed-at, if I may use such a phrase. (It parallels the structure of Folk speech.) I hoped that old Anana's veins would swell up and up and she would die of a stroke.

But I knew that it was the end of the affair that mattered and that I might be dead, or wish I were dead, in a day or two. Or even sooner.

Within fourteen hours, we were getting off a small boat on a beach near Bournemouth, a city of Hampshire County. We walked up a steep flight of wooden steps to the top of a cliff. Four automobiles awaited us. It was four o'clock in the morning, and fog pressed heavily around us. Though the driver of my car could not see where he was going, he seemed to be trusting to instinct. He drove at what was a suicidal clip in the blindness, forty miles per hour, through the streets of Bournemouth. But a radar scope on the dashboard showed ghostly images of cars and people and street lamps and signposts, though we could not read the signs, of course.

Our trip had been smooth and speedy all the way. At Dakar, rather, at a strip in the desert many miles outside Dakar, the metal belt was cut off me and the shell of plastic explosive and the epoxy glue was removed. We were given new clothes and forged papers before transferring to a plane which took us around Spain to a small airport off the coast of southwestern France. From there we took an amphibian which set us down next to a small motor yacht twenty miles off the coast, just outside the fog. If you have enough money and have spent some years in building up your own organization, just in case you have a falling out with the Nine, you find that you can get much done quickly and quietly. As long as I could keep feeding my men money, and I had enough gold stashed away in Africa and elsewhere to do so, I had more than just myself to rely on in this battle. And, of course, Doc Caliban had his own organization, just as he had his own supply of gold.

It pays to be rich, as Clio often told me.

It was still dark and foggy when we were dropped off

before a small hotel outside the city of Salisbury off Highway A338. Clara sat up in bed for a long time smoking until I asked her to quit or else go into the next room. I smoked heavily when I was first introduced to civilization, but that dissipation did not last long. It left too foul a taste and reduced my wind and was a nuisance altogether. Now I could not endure to have smoke anywhere near in an enclosed bedroom.

The maid woke me with a tap on the door at six. Clara was asleep but awoke shortly after I had shaved. She said, "I was trying to think last night why the Nine should be here. I know that they are supposed to have tracked Iwaldi here. But why here? Then I remembered some years ago when I ran into a man I'd only seen twice before, both times at the caves. I was in London then, visiting friends. William Griffin, a son of Lord Braybroke, I believe, told me of overhearing a conversation between a Speaker and his woman. We candidates are great gossips, you know, trying to find out all we can about the Nine. The Speaker had overheard Shaumbim telling Tilatoc that the world had changed so much that it would be impossible to hold funeral rites at some of the places most closely associated with the Nine. Anana's birthplace, for instance, was now covered by a great office building in Spain."

Shaumbim was one of the two Mongolian members of the Nine. Tilatoc was the ancient Central American Indian.

"XauXaz was the one who died. Do you know anything about him at all? Could he have been associated with Stonehenge?"

"I've heard XauXaz speaking in an ancient tongue, some sort of proto-Germanic," I said. "And he spoke to me in English several times when I was Speaker, but only to give orders. Just before Caliban and I were sent from the caves with orders to fight each other to the death, Anana told me a few things about Caliban and myself. We're half-brothers, and our grandfather was XauXaz. He may also have been our great-great-grandfather. God knows how many times he was our ancestor. He used Grandrith Castle as a breeding farm in some kind of experiment. I suspect that his brothers, Ebn XauXaz and Thrithjaz, who are also dead, may have bred the Grandrith family, maybe a long time before the Grandriths came to England, when they were Norsemen. And maybe a long time before then, maybe they started when our ancestors were just forming their Germanic speech. I don't know, I'm guessing. I also suspect that old Ing, he whom the original Old English speakers worshiped as a living god, and he from whose name England was derived, may have taken a part in the breeding of the Grandrith line. Just as I suspect that my being raised by subhumans may have been an experiment of the Nine.

"But I'm digressing. I don't know what XauXaz had to do with Stonehenge. He was at least eighteen thousand five hundred years old when Stonehenge was built and maybe three times as old. He had been associated with the Germanic people from the beginning. And I doubt very much that the builders of Stonehenge, the 'Wessex' peoples, who probably descended from the Bronze Beaker peoples, were Germanic. The proto-Germanic language wouldn't even have existed then.

"But maybe he was associated with the Stonehenge people, maybe he was their living god. Maybe he supervised the building of Stonehenge. And then the Wessex people declined or he left them and went to the land between the Oder and the Elbe rivers. It is possible."

We might never know. But the Nine were here for what must be a very good reason for them.

Murtagh entered with a noticeable increase in the frequency of oscillations of face. His skin was pale, and his mouth was as thin as the edge of a fingernail.

"Are you exceptionally nervous?" I said.

"Exceptionally so," he replied. "But I always am when on the brink of an important action. You will find that my nerve won't desert me. I can be relied upon."

I told him what Clara and I had been discussing and asked him if he had any information.

"The Nine, as you well know, are sticklers for tradition," he said. "I suppose when you've lived as long as they have, you will be, too. Though the way you live I doubt you'll reach even a hundred. No offense!" he added sharply. Apparently, though he had thrown in with me, he still resented me.

"I rather believe that the ceremony will be the burial of XauXaz, if he is associated with this place. Not a genuine burial, because even the Nine don't have enough influence to bury him in the center of Stonehenge and keep all questions suppressed. But the funeral could be held there, and he could be buried nearby in some private land."

It seemed like a sound theory. I started to comment on it when the phone rang. I was closest, so I answered. A strange voice, deep as a hog grunting at the bottom of a well, spoke.

"J.C.? D.C. here!"

It was the proper challenge, and I gave the proper response. "Seedy? Seejay here!"

"Speaking for D.C.," the deep voice said. "Van Veelar. My

friends call me Pauncho. Trish said to say hello. O.K.?"

By that he must have meant that the naming of Trish was an additional reassurance that he was sent by Caliban. Patricia Wilde was Doc's beautiful cousin, whom I was supposed to have killed but who was very much alive, as both Doc and I discovered.

"Meet you at the corner of Barnard and Gigant Streets," he said. "Be smoking a big cigar. You know what *G. beringei* looks like?"

That had to mean gorilla beringei, the mountain gorilla. I said, "Very well."

"That's me. A dead ringer for old beringei. You can't mistake me. Smoking a cigar in a big black Rolls. Always travel in style. See you. Hurry. This line may be tapped. Oh, and don't forget! Anybody with metal fillings in their teeth is out. Or with metal plates in their heads. Or anywhere in their bodies. Right? You got the message? Right!"

There was a click. I passed the word out, and in five minutes we had paid our bill and were driving away. The fog was as thick as ever. The sun was an exceedingly pale halo just above the housetops. The radio said that the fog had been in the area for two days and showed no signs of leaving. It was a freak phenomenon, extending inland for forty miles north of the coast.

I had been to Salisbury twenty years before, but I have a good memory for topography and direction. And we had a city map. So we found the corner of Barnard and Gigant and located the Silver Cloud in an illegal parking area. I approached the car from the sidewalk side while Clara and Murtagh came on him from the street side.

His window was open, and the collar of his thick black coat

was up and his bowler hat was tipped forward. The cigar reeked in the heavy wet air. I bent down to look at him through the window. His profile was much like that of a male of The Folk.

Clara said something to him, and he motioned to me to come into the car. Clara and Murtagh went onto the sidewalk side and leaned in to hear through the window on the side, which he had opened. He turned on the ceiling lights. His eyebrows were the thickest I'd ever seen. His nose was a smudge; his upper lip was proportionately as long as an orangutan's; his jaws protruded; his teeth were thick but widely spaced. The eyes under those heavy supraorbital ridges were small and gray-blue. Despite his intense ugliness, he radiated likableness.

"Doc told me all about you," he said. "I don't know anything about our gang, but he said that you were the boss at your end of things, so I'm your obedient servant. I think we'd better get going, 'cause time is of the essence. You got pocket communicators so you can tell 'em back here to stick close to us. Easy to get lost in this soup."

I showed him the cigarette-lighter shaped transceivers which had a range of a half-mile. He was familiar with them, since Caliban had invented them. We got into the cars, I gave orders, and the four cars started up close on Pauncho's rear bumper. He had exceptionally long arms, and the body under the coat was keg-shaped. He talked out of the side of his mouth while the cigar bobbed up and down.

"I ain't got time to tell you everything that happened in Germany. Suffice it that we've tracked Iwaldi to this area. He's here because he knew the Nine would be holding XauXaz's funeral. They're on to his being here. They are also on to us being here, but all they know, so far, is that we are in the area, too. They've been looking for us; we've had some narrow escapes here. But that's all polluted water under the bridge. Listen, watch the road signs, will you? We got to take A-three-six-o northwest out of town. I made a dry run last night, but in this fog... whoops! Watch it, you crazy fool!"

A dark form swerved away from us, its horn blaring.

"Listen, the radio last night interviewed some crackpot that claimed this fog was caused by witches. Said there was a coven lived near Stonehenge. I ain't so sure he was too far off the beam. Doc says old Anana has some strange powers that reach way back into the Old Stone Age. But I'm getting off the track. Here's the shape-up. Doc and Trish—what a dish!—and Barney, my dumb-dumb buddy, are near Stonehenge, by the long barrows at the crossing of A-three-six-o and A-three-o-three. Doc says if they're gone when we get there, we should proceed on to Stonehenge. The ceremony'll take place sometime today. The Nine won't be bothered by tourists on account of the fog or the local police. They've pulled strings to assure that. Doc thinks the police have been told that the British secret service wants the area kept clear while they run down enemy agents there. It's easy when you figure that some of the biggest big shots on Downing Street are servants of the Nine."

Pauncho added that Iwaldi was in the neighborhood, though Doc and his aides had not actually seen him. The battle would be three-way with my forces and Doc's definitely in the minority. But our strategy was to hit and run. If we could get just one of the Nine, we would feel happy.

Pauncho van Veelar told us to open the small chests on the

floors. We did so and brought out chain mail shirts and loinguards and close-fitting helmets. All were of irradiated plastic.

"Put them on now," he said. "Once we get there, you won't have much time to change. Those shirts, by the way, resist a direct impact to a considerable degree. But if a man is strong enough—I am—he can tear the links apart."

We started to undress in the cramped quarters. I said, "Doc's message was rather curt. It said not to bring anyone with metal fillings in their teeth or with metal anywhere in their bodies. Now that I see this plastic armor, I'm beginning to get a vague idea of what was behind that cryptic order. Would you mind explaining so our mental fog isn't as thick as that out there?"

"Yeah, sure," he grunted. "Sorry. One thing at a time, I always say. You see, one of Doc's inventions is an inductive-field generator. It sends out a fan-shaped beam with an extreme range of half a mile. It's atomic-powered and eats up a lot of power but an amplifier enables it to radiate almost as much as it takes in. It heats up all metals within its field. Teeth fillings, rings, various articles such as watches, guns, knives, you name it. Copper telephone wires and aluminum high-tension power lines melt, and the towers get too hot to take hold of. The gas in a car's tank will explode from the heat of the metal.

"But we got weapons that we can use in a field in our trunks. Clubs—baseball bats—and plastic knives okay for stabbing but lousy for cutting. And small fiberglass crossbows with gut strings and wooden bolts with plastic points. And plastic grenades with compressed gas and detonators in them. Gunpowder, TNT, cordite, all types of explosives, become very unstable so you can't use them in plastic firearms or bombs. Even the gas in Doc's grenades is a special type of gas."

"So it's back to the primitive?" I said. "I like that."

It was ironic that the servants of the Nine and I had fought each other in the primeval forests of remotest Africa with helicopters, napalm bombs, automatic rifles, personnel detectors, and every up-to-date weapon available. Yet here in one of the most technologically advanced and most populated nations of the world, we were to engage in battle with clubs and knives and tiny bows. And with this heavy fog, we were liable to end up using only the clubs and knives and, indubitably, our hands and feet.

"Except for the materials, the weapons'll be primitive," Pauncho said. "And the inductor prevents the use of personnel radar or other detectors in this fog, too! The Nine'll have their own inductor going, you can bet on that, and the same kind of weapons we'll have, all of which Doc invented. And maybe Iwaldi'll have his inductor on, if he really shows. Of course, he won't unless he's crazy, but he's crazy, no doubt of that. The Nine'll have an army of thugs, and they'll be using them as a big net to catch Iwaldi, not to mention us, if they win the battle, that is.

"Oh, by the way, we'll have to hoof it a mile or so. We can't take the cars inside the inductor area. But Doc says that the Nine'll have cars, enough to carry them inside the area. They got three. Steam driven and plastic. Doc made them for the old geezers for just such a setup as this. Antipoetic justice, ain't it? We ride shank's mare, and they ride in style in cars Doc's genius built for them!"

We got onto A360, and Pauncho pushed the car at eighty all the way. He talked without letup. Ordinarily, such chatter would have rasped my nerves, but he provided much information which I desired. He told me that he was the son of "Jocko" Simmons and that Barney Banks, his *dumb-dumb buddy,* was the son of "Porky" Rivers. These were the old men who had accompanied Doc Caliban on their last adventure at the age of eighty. I have described them and their heroic deaths in Volume IX of my memoirs. They were the last survivors of a group of five who had dedicated their lives to helping Caliban in his battle against evildoers. (Never mind that Caliban was also working for the Nine because they offered him immortality. Caliban was given a free hand to battle crime as long as he did not interfere with the Nine. I do not condemn him for that; I succumbed to the temptation of immortality, too.)

Pauncho and Barney were born in 1932, shortly after their mothers divorced their fathers. Rivers and Simmons spent too much time with their leader and their wives, fed up, cut loose.

"I remember my father, the old ape, visiting me now and then," Pauncho said. "My mother remarried about two years after the divorce, and her husband adopted me. He was a great guy. But I was torn. I liked my father at the same time I hated him because he had, in a sense, deserted me. Now I can appreciate why he decided in favor of adventure. But I loathed chemistry even though my father was one of the world's greatest chemists. Maybe because of that."

Pauncho remembered visits from his "Uncle Doc" and visits to his wonderland laboratory in the eyrie of the Empire State Building. Pauncho and Barney had grown up together, since they lived three houses apart. They were in the same outfit in the Marines during the Korean War. They were visiting Doc after the deaths of their fathers, when he invited them to join him. Both had apparently inherited a love for adventure and combat from their fathers, and when they found out that Doc's own researches were close to the point where he would be able to reproduce the immortality elixir, they accepted his offer.

At the rate Pauncho was going, we would have reached the junction of the two highways in ten minutes. But we had to stop to avoid running into a pile-up of three cars. He slowed down to forty after that. Then, after a glance at the milometer, he crept along until the junction suddenly moved out from the fog. He turned right and drove for a few feet and then parked the car on the side of the road. The other cars followed. Two of the drivers got out swearing about the crazy fool Yank.

I could see no more than a few feet, but I knew that the country for miles around was as flat as Illinois farmland. A303 ran like a cannon barrel slightly northwest for about a mile and a quarter before crossing an untarred road. To get to Stonehenge, you turned left onto the untarred road and went about an eighth of a mile before passing Stonehenge, which was behind a fence in a field. At the junction of A344 and the small road, you turned left and then almost immediately were at the entrance to the "venerable and stupendous work on Salisbury Plain, vulgarly ascribed to Merlin, the Prophet," as described by John Wood, architect of Bath, in 1747.

If the air had been clear, we would have been able to see the white chalk wherever the soil had been cut away.

Pauncho got out of the car and removed his heavy overcoat. Since I was only a foot from him, I was able to see how he got his nickname. His belly stuck out as round as a gorilla's after a heavy meal of bamboo shoots. But it gave the impression of being as hard as a gorilla's chest. His arms were freakishly long, and his legs were very short. Even so, he stood six feet high, unlike his father, who had been not quite five feet high. Pauncho looked as if he weighed three hundred and twenty pounds or so.

He opened the trunk of his car and passed out the weapons to us. I took a baseball bat, a plastic seven-inch long stiletto, which I put in a sheath at my belt, a short quiver of bolts, also hung from my belt, and a crossbow. This was small and held with one hand, like a pistol, when fired. The bowstring was pulled back by hand, requiring a strong man to pull it all the way back. A catch secured the string, both of which were released when the trigger just ahead of the pistol-like butt was pulled.

"If the string is set at the extreme of the three positions and shot within a range of three feet," Pauncho said, "the bow will send a bolt through the armor we're wearing. Not very far, probably not more'n a half-inch into your flesh. But that'll smart, and if the bolt hits unprotected flesh, it'll go almost all the way through you."

The grenades looked like tennis balls. From the top of each protruded a half-inch long pin.

"Twist the pin to the left as far as it'll go. Pull the pin and then throw," Pauncho said. "Don't dillydally. Six seconds later, the mingling of two gases produces an explosion equivalent to one and a quarter pound of TNT. The plastic shell is almost atomized, so these depend on concussion for main effect."

Two steps behind him, I followed Pauncho into the field. We sprang over a fence, the wire of which was warming up under the inductor's field, and walked a few steps. He stopped.

The mound of the barrow had loomed out of the fog. Pauncho called softly, "Hey, Doc! It's me, Pauncho!"

There was no answer. The others, fanning out around the barrow, called quietly. I went up and over the mound and then along its other side. There was no one there. By bending down with my eyes close to the grass, I could see footprints in the wet earth.

We returned to the cars. Pauncho swore and blew on his enormous hands. "It's cold! That fog goes right through my bones!"

He called out, "Hey, Countess! You any good at warming up a man?"

Clara laughed softly and said, "You could chase me, my pithecanthropoid friend. That would warm you up! But save your strength!"

"We'll talk this over a martini sometime," he rumbled.

"I'll meet you after the fight," she said.

"Wait'll I tell that would-be-swinger, Barney, about this," Pauncho said, and he chuckled like a troll under a bridge.

I said, "Silence!"

Shouts were drifting through the gray wetness. Muffled cracks, as of bats striking bats or armor or, perhaps, bone, disturbed the cloud.

I called them in around me and told them what we should do for the moment. We started out just as a few more cracking noises came and then a scream which was cut off as if a knife had plunged into the throat. A grenade boomed three seconds later. Then silence returned.

If there were many people at Stonehenge, they were not conducting a full-scale battle. The sounds gave us the impression of blundering around, of probing activity by men who were not sure even after they had closed with another whether he was enemy or friend.

"We'll walk along the road until we're just opposite the first of the tumuli."

"What the hell's a tumuli?" someone muttered.

"A tumulus is an artificial mound, a round barrow," I said. "A grave for the ancients. This area is filled with them. We'll scout around there, take it easy, because Iwaldi or the Nine may have stationed people there. Keep close together. We don't want to get separated in this fog. Yes, I know bunching makes us better targets, but that can't be helped.

"And don't fire at the first person you see. He may be one of Doc's people. Now you've gotten the descriptions of Doc and Banks and his cousin. If you can identify them, sing out and identify yourself. Pongo is the code word."

"Identify them? In this fog soup?" a man muttered.

"Do your best," I said. "Outside of Caliban's group, everybody is our enemy."

I did not really expect Murtagh's men to refrain from shooting until they were one hundred percent certain. They were all very tough and self-centered characters, and they were not about to wait until hit before they opened up. But at least they knew what their allies were supposed to look like.

We walked on the edge of the road with me in the lead. I held the butt of the crossbow in my right hand and the bat in my left.

The sounds had ceased but as soon as we reached the burial barrow three explosions deafened us. All of us dived for the wet ground, even though there was no indication that the grenades were being thrown our way. Then I rose, and, crouching, ran to the ditch around the outer wall of the barrow and dived into it. I fell on top of a man squatting on his heels. He grunted, I grunted, and I broke his jaw with a backhanded blow from the butt end of my bat.

Somebody nearby in the fog said, "What the hell is that? You all right, Meeters?"

The man I'd knocked out was not named Meeters, because he answered on my left about ten feet away.

At that moment Clara and Pauncho appeared in the fog, so I jumped up, yelling, and started swinging with the bat. I kept hold of the crossbow, which was loaded, until I was facing two at one time. One I shot through the mouth with the bolt and the other I knocked down with a blow that broke my bat, his bat, and his skull under his helmet.

I think I cleared the ditch on my side. But there were men on the other side of the barrow. Instead of charging around the ditch or coming over the top of the barrow, they took off. Somewhere in the fog some of them got down on the ground and began firing bolts back. All these did was to bury themselves in the dirt of the mound. But we scrambled into the ditch as if they could hit us. And of course they might flank us.

While I checked for dead or wounded among us, and found that only two of us were out of the fight, Murtagh and Pauncho examined the enemy. All ten were dead or unconscious. But there was no way of determining if they were Iwaldi's or the Nine's. They were dressed in civilian clothes with a bright yellow band pinned across their chests. All had plastic chain mail shirts under cloth shirts, plastic loinguards, and helmets shaped exactly like ours.

Gbampwe, a black from Central Africa who said he was a champion spear thrower, and I cast grenades into the fog. I threw mine with a force which should have taken them about four hundred feet. They opened up the fog with a red roar. I couldn't tell if I hit anything because the only reply was a volley of bolts, some of which hit the soft earth of the barrow above us.

Somebody far away called. I could not make out the words, which were either garbled by the atmospheric conditions or were purposely distorted.

I bellowed, "Pongo! Pongo! Pongo!"

"Pongo your...!" somebody yelled, his last words lost in an uproar of shouts and screams and cracking bats.

Pauncho growled, "The farmers around here must be screaming their heads off for the police. And I'll bet they can hear those grenades clear on the other side of Amesbury. It's only two miles away."

It must have been a strain on the local police to give excuses for the explosions and for the loss of power. They must have wondered themselves just what the secret service was doing out around Stonehenge. But they would, of course, obey their orders. I took it for granted that the same orders had gone to the armed service posts in this area, of which there were many.

I threw another grenade. It went off almost exactly between the locations of the two previous blasts. Bolts whistled nearby after the explosion, but none struck us. It seemed reasonable that I might have killed the men we'd run out of the ditch, and that these missiles came from another group. On the other hand, they might be holding their fire, hoping we would think just that.

To our right, approximately at Stonehenge, another flurry of cracking noises came muffled through the fog.

I gave the order to get out of the ditch and to advance across the field. We would go parallel with the road on a course which would bring us near the so-called "slaughter stone." This lies outside the circle of the trilithons and sarsens and near the heel stone, which is named thus for no verifiable reason.

Suddenly, there was not a sound except for the rustle of our feet moving through the wet winter weeds and a slight sucking as feet were pulled up from mud. We were formed in three lines. I was in the lead with Clara, Pauncho, and Murtagh behind me at the limits of my sight. If I had stepped up my pace a trifle, I would have been all alone, as far as my ability to see was concerned. About halfway to the slaughter stone, or at a point which I believed to be halfway, I threw up my hand. The three behind me also signaled, and then the whole body was at rest. There was no more sound than if we had been at the bottom of a deep cave.

The only thing you could hear was the hum of nervous tension.

Out there were many men moving slowly, their eyes straining against the gray cloud, their breaths controlled, their feet descending and ascending slowly to avoid the suck of mud and brush of wet grass. Their ears were turning this way and that to catch a betraying sound.

My hearing and sense of smell are far keener than most humans, for reasons which I have explained in Volume II of my memoirs. But there was not a breath of wind, and the heavy droplet-ridden cloud seemed to be killing both sound and odor. I had a mental picture of enemy all around us, men who, if they knew where we were, could have cut us down with their crossbows or overwhelmed us with numbers alone. The blindness was to our advantage because of our very small force.

I gestured for us to advance. And then I heard a poofing sound, which I interpreted immediately, and correctly, as it turned out. I turned and gave the signal to hit the earth and then did so.

No sooner had I hugged the earth than an intensely bright light shot through the cloud above us. Somebody had sent up a flare. It had to be entirely nonmetallic, of course.

It did not turn night into day, but it did outline a mass of figures beyond the depression in which was the slaughter stone. And it showed me some vague figures gathered around the somewhat tilted sixteen-foot high heel stone to my right near the road.

There were six or more ahead and about eight to the right. None of them made the signal agreed upon if visibility should be restored.

But they had seen us stretched out on the ground. They had also seen each other.

We fired crossbow bolts back at both groups as they fired at us and at each other.

That seemed to be a signal for bedlam. Beyond, in the gray mists around the circle of Stonehenge, grenades opened the fog with flames. Men behind me screamed, and men ahead of me screamed.

And then there was silence again except for the groans of the wounded. These were shut up as quickly as we could with our hands over their mouths and then with morphine. I suppose the other groups had done the same, because I could not hear any wounded from any quarter.

Silence again.

If those two groups had not moved... I lobbed two grenades in quick order at where I thought they should be. The blasts came one after the other. There were screams and moans after the reverberations had died away. Then answering blasts, the flashes of which I could not see. The wounded quit making noises. By then I was up, crouching, and had told my men to follow me to the left, across the field. I was afraid that those not hit would retaliate with grenades. And while I doubted that anyone of them could throw a grenade as far as I had, we would still be within stunning range. Or one of them might run forward and toss the grenade.

It was a mistake on my part. A dark body suddenly appeared ahead of me, a crossbow string twanged, others near it let loose, and about six of my men, as I was to find out, were killed. I went down but not because I was shot. I fell forward, shooting my crossbow as I went. After I had hit the earth, I reloaded my weapon. The men ahead were silenced, and when I crawled forward, cautiously, I found three corpses and one wounded, unconscious. He had a bright yellow strip, splashed with blood, across his chest. I put him out of his misery with my stiletto.

Our outburst triggered off another in the vicinity of the ruins. Bolts whistled overhead. I think they were strays, but even so, one caught one of my men in the neck.

I crawled on and came across the first of many bodies within a narrow area. I counted twenty-five.

"Listen!" I said to Pauncho. "I don't know what is going on. But I doubt that any of the Nine would expose themselves as we have. They value their wrinkled hides far too much. But they must have come here because they would want to bring Iwaldi out in the open. And they *will* take chances. So they have to be here. I wonder if they could have exposed themselves long enough to bring Iwaldi's men out and then cut and run for it? Or they could be holed up in their cars."

But, cautious as they were, they were not cowards. And they were completists. They would want to make sure that Iwaldi had been killed. And if they knew that there were other forces operating in the grayness, they would be certain that these would be Doc or I or both. They would not rest until our heads had been brought before them.

I said, "I'm going to go back to the road and scout along it. You come along as far as the fence. Stay there for twenty minutes. If I'm not back by then, it's up to you what you do."

"Doc probably needs our help!" Pauncho said. "There are a hell of a lot of men out there!"

As if to prove his statement, the fog was shattered with three grenade explosions somewhere to our left. And then we heard the whoosh of several bolts very near us. Somebody was shooting at random.

Clara wormed to me and said, "I want to go with you, John! I proved I can fight along with you!"

"All right," I said. "Let's make for the fence."

"Doc said I was to be under your orders while I was with you," Pauncho said. "But he told me I could rejoin him as soon as I got the chance. Well, now I got the chance. And that dumb-dumb Barney, he'd fall down and break his leg if I wasn't there to hold him up. And Doc may need me. No telling what's going on out there."

"You do whatever you think best," I said. I appreciated his loyalty and his concern for his comrades, and he had carried out his mission: to get us to the battlefield.

"Yeah, I'd like to stick with you, but I got a hunch they really need me," Pauncho said. "So long. Good luck."

He crawled away. I led the others to the road and ended up by the heel stone. This tilted to the south as if it were an ancient tombstone and the earth around it had yielded up its dead. Ten corpses lay around it. I looked them over and determined that about five had been killed by a blast, presumably from the grenade I had thrown. These men had yellow bands across their chests.

Murtagh said, "I would prefer that we all go together. If we don't, we're likely to end up shooting each other in this damned fog!"

At that moment, the firing stopped again for a few seconds, a pistol fired, there was some shouting, and then silence.

I said, "Clara and I'll go down the road. If you hear firing down there, stay here. I'll give you the code word when I come back. Pauncho knows where you are, so if he finds Doc he may bring them here."

Clara and I started to go down the dirt along the right side of the road. We had gone only a few feet when I heard the tires of a car accelerating swiftly, near the vicinity of the crossroads. There was no sound of a motor, so I knew it was a steam-driven car. And immediately after, grenades broke loose across the road from us. I don't know that they were throwing them directly at us on purpose, because they could not have seen across the road. But Murtagh and his men lobbed their grenades back across the road, and then suddenly figures loomed out of the fog. The roar of the car increased, and then I felt a hard blow against my chest. I looked down, dimly saw a grenade at my feet, leaned down and threw it back. It went off in the air and the grayness became black.

When I recovered consciousness, I was lying on my side on the cold wet earth. My ears rang, and my head felt as if it had swelled to pumpkin size. I put my hand on my head and felt a stickiness. I tasted my fingers. It was blood running out from a small cut on my throbbing head.

The noise level around me must have been high, because surely there were men screaming and groaning. Two bodies lay within touching distance, and when I got to my hands and knees and began crawling around, feeling for a club or a crossbow, I came across three more corpses. I found a crossbow and a quiver containing six bolts on a still body. I got to my feet and staggered across the road, stumbled over another body, fell down into a small depression, crawled out, and stopped. Something large and black and metallic-feeling was blocking my way.

I pulled myself up onto it, and then my senses, slowly clearing, told me it was the plastic steam car. It was lying on its side; the doors on the upper side were open. I looked into it and saw one body huddled down against the lower side in the back. I looked up across the car and saw a few flashes, like fireflies on a broad meadow. They were from grenade explosions, but I could not hear a thing.

Prowling around the car in the milky fog, I found a man in a chauffeur's uniform face-down on the road. He had been hit on the head with a bat and then stabbed in the throat.

I went back to the car. I hated to be trapped inside it, but I had to find out who that was in the rear seat. I climbed up and into the well with less than my usual suppleness and strength. The explosion had taken much out of me. By the corpse, I lit a match and shone it on the face for a moment.

He was one of the Mongolian members of the Nine, withered old Jiizfan. Those eyes, which had been young when there was still a land bridge between England and the continent, were closed. There was no sign of a wound except a dark mark on his forehead.

I put my ear against his chest and heard nothing. Then I placed a thumb on his skinny wrist and detected a very light pulse.

I raised my head and looked into the ragged pits of his eyes.

His hand moved. I caught it and squeezed. The bones ground together, and he screamed out.

It was a pitiful cry, but he had been responsible for the deaths of thousands, perhaps millions, during his multi-millennia-long life. God alone knew how many he had tortured. And he would have had me killed instantly if it was in his power.

I turned on the flashlight for just a moment, shining it on my face so he could see who it was. Then I cast the beam in his face. His eyes were wide open, his mouth was sagging.

Before I could reach up and twist his neck, his hand fell back and he slumped down. I felt his pulse. His heart had given out on seeing me.

However, a man who has lived that long, especially for so long in the Orient, may conceivably be able to stop his own heart for a while through mental means. When I climbed out, I carried his head by the long white hair. I wasn't sure what I was going to do with it. Toss it among his men if I could find them, I suppose. But I laid it down by the car while I investigated, and I never did pick it up again.

From the wounds on the bodies around the car, and the bashed-in rear, and the skid marks, I reconstructed the accident. Just as the men had charged across the road, to attack us or to run away from attackers, the lead car had plowed in among them. It had knocked several high into the air but its wheels had struck several bodies on the road, and it had turned over. It must have been going about sixty miles an hour when it hit. The car behind it had run over some bodies and rammed the rear of the first car just as it turned over on its side. Then the second car had backed up and taken off.

The occupants of the wrecked car, except for Jiizfan, had managed to crawl out, assisted by the chauffeur. (I suddenly remembered seeing him at one of the annual ceremonies.) He had been shot down, perhaps by his own people in the fog. The others, who I presumed were of the Nine, had gotten away. Whether they had gotten into the second car or were walking along the road through the fog was something I could only determine if I went after them.

I did not know how long I had been unconscious. I did not know whether or not Clara or Doc were within a few feet and shouting out the code word.

I circled around and around and found all of my party dead except for Clara, Murtagh, and Szeleszny. The attack that had gotten me must have gotten them, too. One of the corpses was carrying a quiver with several bolts. I fitted one to my bow, picked up a bat, checked that I still had my knife and two grenades. The fog, which had started to turn whitish, was much darker. Apparently, above the fog, other clouds had moved in.

I went down the route I had started before being so violently interrupted. My head still felt as if somebody were pumping a very painful gas into it. My ears had not stopped ringing.

The fog became less dark again as I came to the junction of the two roads. I turned around in the slowly whitening mists to the left and cut across the road. Moving along the road on my right, I came to the entrance to the ruins. By then the ringing in my ears was not so loud, and my head did not feel quite so much like a balloon. But it still hurt.

Out of the thick milkiness, dark figures appeared, one by one. They were corpses on the white chalky path before me. Between the entrance at the northeast corner of the field and the flat stone at the perimeter of the ruins, just beyond the end of the path, I counted thirty-three bodies. I did not stop to investigate all of them, but many that I did had caved-in skulls, broken necks, or shattered jaws. Those with no marks of violence except swollen heads, bulging eyes, and bloody issues from nose, eye, and ear were the victims of grenades.

I stood for a while by the flat stone and tried to listen. I also sniffed the air, but could smell nothing but a wet wooliness. Then I advanced slowly to the left until two flat stones bulked out of the mist. These were broken stones lying on their sides. If I remembered correctly, just beyond the farthest was the first of the upright monoliths of the "gigantick pile." A few steps showed me that my memory had not failed me. The blackish-gray tablet seemed to drift out of the fog as if it were the mast of a stone ship.

Three bodies lay between its foot and the flat stone by it.

I determined, while I stood there, straining my senses to detect living bodies in the cloud, to go to the right, toward the center of the inner circle of trilithons and monolith. There the funeral ceremony for XauXaz would have been held, if the Nine had been allowed to hold it. And there his body might still be, if the Nine had been routed.

Then, to my right, a body did emerge from the milkiness. It put one foot before the other while it leaned forward, straining to see. It held something in front of it which, a second later, I saw was her crossbow.

We moved closer. Her bow was up, and her finger was ready to squeeze the trigger, and then she recognized me.

I did not speak because I did not want anyone else to hear us. And I could not hear Clara. I would have to read her lips, which would not be easy in the syrupiness.

Something came down out of the cloud. It seemed to have dropped from an airplane, but it must have been crouched on top of the monolith to my left, about fourteen feet high. It landed hard and rolled and disappeared and then was up on its feet and bounding toward Clara. She had jumped back, almost disappearing from my sight, and then she came forward again but with her right side turned to me. She loosed the arrow at the monstrous figure, which had been swallowed by the fog again but which she must have seen because she was closer.

Then the hulking shape leaped out of the fog as if vomited by it, grabbed her arm, went on, turning her upsidedown and then over. I ran up to her. I was too late. Her right arm had been twisted and torn off, along with the jacket and the chain mail shirt, by the enormous strength of that brute. The dark blood gushed out over the white chalk. She was dead.

My beautiful and brave and loving Clara was dead.

Her sudden death and its manner froze me. But I was additionally horrified because of the unexpectedness of the creature's appearance. I had thought that Dick was in Central Africa, waiting for me to return.

I did not know how he had gotten here, but the Nine had to have something to do with it. He had gotten into contact with them, and they had decided to use him against me instead of killing him. They needed somebody who was stronger than I and knew all the techniques of hand and foot fighting. And who, in an arena where gunpowder and metal were forbidden, would be like a lion loose. A lion with the mind of a man.

And while I stood over her and was as motionless and as dumb as those ancient piles around me, the huge shape dived out of the fog.

I went down. But, before he touched me, I came out of the horror as if I had been slid down a greased chute. I went onto my back and my feet kicked up. The bat and the crossbow were flung to one side. His hands were over my face—they would have taken my face off if they could have gotten a grip—and he went on over me and into the fog, propelled by the impact of my feet on the underside of his great paunch.

I grabbed the bat—the crossbow was lost in the mists— and I got on my feet and was ready when he came out of the wooliness again. But this time he was feet first, his body almost parallel with the ground, and those short but gorilla-powerful legs bent. They straightened out, and if they had hit my chest would have broken the bones. They did hit the club with enough force to knock it from my hands.

I rolled back and away into the fog and came down hard because I had not been fully prepared for that type of attack and I had slipped in Clara's blood.

He came down on Clara's body, then disappeared.

I was up and heading toward where I hoped the nearest monolith would be. I wanted to get my back to it, get my feet against it, and then launch myself at him, if he showed again. There was the chance that we would blunder by each other, perhaps not see each other again in this place. But his hearing was, as far as I knew, unaffected, and mine was still absent. That gave him an advantage. I wanted to stay in one spot, where he could not approach me from the rear, and wait for him. Even my breathing would have to be silent; I controlled the urge to suck in deep breaths.

At the foot of the rough pillar, blackish in the fog, the toe of my shoe nudged something. I knelt down and felt it. It was Clara's arm, thrown aside by the anthropoid.

I picked it up by the wrist with my right hand and drew my stiletto with my left hand. I waited. I could see about a foot before me. I wondered if there were sounds of a frantic battle going on around me. Perhaps Doc Caliban or his men or Trish Wilde or Murtagh were crying for aid only a few feet from me.

Suddenly, I smelled him. He had to be very close for me to detect him in the thick-dropleted cloud. And he would, of course, smell me.

I swung the arm as hard as I could before me, and it slapped his dark shoving-forward face just as it came like a black ghost out of the mists. But a powerful blow from him struck my wrist and knocked the stiletto into the mists.

The force of the blow from Clara's arm squeezed more blood out of it over his face. It blinded him, disconcerted him, and so the club he swung in his left hand missed me and broke against the stone where I had been. And I came up with my left fist with all my force into his belly, exactly against the wound I had given him on that mountain road in Africa.

He bent forward, clutching at his belly, and I slammed my right fist behind his left ear. He sagged forward and went down on his knees, and I hit the back side of that huge massively muscled neck with the edge of my palm.

If he had been a man, he would have died. But he was only half-stunned, and he came up and around with his right hand in a karate chop—though I think it was purely a reflex—and my left arm felt as if it, too, had been torn off.

The agony would come later. At that moment, the arm was numbed. I also hurt my knee so much that I could only hobble for a long time after that. But it was worth it.

He fell face-down, and I thought he surely must be dead. But he rolled over while I stared at him and I bit my lips to keep from groaning with the agony of my knee and my left arm. I stared while he got to a sitting position. I started forward, determined to kick him with my left foot, though I did not know how I could stand on my right while I was doing it. He looked at me moving through the fog at him and then he fell back and stared upward. Suspecting a trick, I circled him, with difficulty since I could not move without great pain. I approached him from behind. He did not move. Then I knelt down, again with difficulty, and closed my one good hand around his throat. I began to squeeze. His eyes opened. His tongue came out. He rolled his head slightly, but his arms did not move. And then that enormous chest quit rising and falling.

It could as easily have been me on the ground and probably would have been if he had not skidded in Clara's blood.

I released my hold on his throat and turned away. At that moment, announced by a grenade exploding in the distance, as if some dramatist in the sky had arranged matters, the first breeze cooled my face. The wind increased as I walked toward the inner circle of the ruins, and within a few strides I could see several feet away.

There were bodies everywhere, clubs, bows, arrows, and plastic knives. Murtagh was not among them.

In the center, lying on his back, his arms crossed, was XauXaz.

His catafalque was of ornately carved oak with affixed golden images. His enormous white beard covered his chest and his stomach. The old wide-brimmed floppy hat lay above his head; his right eye was covered with a black patch held on by a thin black band. A huge black raven sat on each shoulder.

As I approached, they flew away, crying harshly.

Beyond, over the body, the mists were thinning.

There were more corpses past the trilithons.

I stood by the body of my grandfather, of the man who may have fathered many times in the Grandrith line, the millennia-old man who had once been worshiped as a god, as Wothenjaz by the first Germanic speakers, then as Wothen and Othinn and Wodan. The Mad One. He had many names, but in the caves of the Nine, he was called XauXaz, which meant, in proto-Germanic, High. And his brothers were Ebn XauXaz, or Just-As-High, and Thrithjaz, or Third. All dead now.

Soon the mists would be blown away. And the rude and massive and brooding stones would be revealed on this level land. And there would be visible this ancient, very ancient oaken catafalque and the body of the man who looked as if he were a hundred years old but had actually been born sometime between 10,000 B.C. and 20,000 B.C. And there would be the body of a creature that science had thought had perished a million and a half years ago. And there would be the other bodies, and the primitive weapons by which they had perished, the clubs and the bows and arrows with plastic tips and the plastic daggers.

Unless the Nine arranged to keep the area shut long enough to have the bodies hauled away, and all speculation hushed up, the story of the battle at Stonehenge would go around the world. And the mystery would be pondered on for years. Perhaps for as long as men were on this planet.

But I knew the Nine, and I knew that those who had gotten away, old Anana and Ing and the others, would arrange to cover up everything.

In fact, if I did not get out at once, I might be caught in the net they had undoubtedly spread to drag in all who would try to leave this area.

I hobbled past the great stones and out across the field. I thought I had seen, for a brief moment when the mists had parted, a number of bicycles on the edge of the field. These would be plastic, of course, and might have been brought here by Caliban. If I could pedal one of these, though handicapped by a useless left arm and a knee which it was agony to bend, then I could get to a car. I might have to steal one, but I knew how to do this, even though born and bred in the jungle.

It was then the fog split, and I saw the giant figure of a man with a peculiar bronzish hair and skin. By his side was a tall woman with the same coloring and a man with grotesquely broad shoulders and long arms, Pauncho. There were four men and a woman I did not recognize.

Bodies lay near them.

I hurried toward him, then had to slow down because of the pain.

Doc had stopped and was waiting for me. Then, seeing I was in such trouble, he ran toward me.

I smiled for the first time in a long time. We had gotten through, and we would get away. I would find out what had happened to Clio. And then we would go to the mountains which conceal the caves of the Nine and there do what had to be done.

SHERLOCK HOLMES

BY GUY ADAMS

The Breath of God

A body is found crushed to death in the London snow. There are no footprints anywhere near. It is almost as if the man was killed by the air itself. This is the first in a series of attacks that sees a handful of London's most prominent occultists murdered. While pursuing the case, Holmes and Watson have to travel to Scotland to meet with the one person they have been told can help: Aleister Crowley.

The Army of Doctor Moreau

Following the trail of several corpses seemingly killed by wild animals, Holmes and Watson stumble upon the experiments of Doctor Moreau. Determined to prove Darwin's evolutionary theories, through vivisection and crude genetic engineering Moreau is creating animal hybrids. In his laboratory, Moreau is building an army of 'beast men' in order to gain control of the government…

CAPTAIN NEMO

The Fantastic Adventures of a Dark Genius

BY KEVIN J. ANDERSON

When André Nemo's father dies suddenly, the young adventurer takes to the sea and is accompanied by his lifelong friend, Jules Verne. Verne is thwarted in his yearning for action, while Nemo continues to travel across continents…

THE MARTIAN WAR

BY KEVIN J. ANDERSON

What if the Martian invasion was not entirely the product of H. G. Wells's vivid imagination? What if Wells witnessed something that spurred him to write *The War of the Worlds* as a warning? From drafty London flats to the steamy Sahara, to the surface of the moon and beyond, *The Martian War* takes the reader on an exhilarating journey with Wells and his companions.

In these original novels, *New York Times* bestselling author Kevin J. Anderson takes the reader on two exhilarating journeys with a host of well-known literary and historical figures.